THE GREAT HOUSE

Lady Ainsley looked up from her spinning (p. 103).

THE GREAT HOUSE

Written and illustrated

by

CYNTHIA HARNETT

METHUEN & CO. LTD. LONDON

36 Essex Street, Strand, W.C.2

First Published September 29th, 1949
Reprinted twice
Reprinted 1960

I.4

CATALOGUE NO. 5122/u

PRINTED IN GREAT BRITAIN BY
BRADFORD AND DICKENS, LONDON W.C.I
AND BOUND BY JAMES BURN & CO. LTD., ESHER

The Street

Chapter One

IT was daylight when Barbara woke up, and already there was a clatter of milk pails and a rumble of wheels on the cobbled street outside. Barbara uncurled and stretched herself in the four-poster bed. She was alone. Aunt Anne, who slept with her, was up and dressed and gone downstairs. It was lovely to lie there and remember that something nice was going to happen to-day. For to-day she and Geoffrey were going with Father, away from noisy, smelly London back to the green country.

The sounds in the street were growing louder. Besides the *Milk O* of the milkmaids, there were now the cries of men selling vegetables or fish or small coals, the creaking of yokes and buckets as serving girls fetched water for the household, the yells of drovers bringing their beasts in to the meat market, and above it all the squealing of a poor frightened pig who seemed to know that he would soon be bacon.

It dawned on Barbara that the light between the thick curtains did not look like sunshine. Was it raining? It seemed always to be raining in London, and then the streets became rivers of evil-smelling mud. There was mud in the country too, of course, but that was clean mud, and everything smelled sweet after rain. It would be dreadful if it rained to-day, because they were going on horseback. Geoffrey was going to ride a horse of his own, and Barbara was to ride pillion behind Father.

She could bear the suspense no longer, so she climbed out of her warm nest in the big bed and pattered across the cold floor. She knelt on the window-seat, pressing her nose against the glass. It was one of the new-fashioned windows with a sash that pulled up and down, and she hated it because it was too heavy for her to open. The windows of the house in the country at Pinner where she had lived when Mother was alive were all casements, and she could undo the latch and lean out whenever she wanted to. But these new-fangled windows were high and light, and she felt like a prisoner inside them. The rooms were high and light too; there were no beamed ceilings or dark corners near the fire where one could be cosy. Father was building nothing but these ugly houses made of garish red brick, for Father was an architect. He said that the new houses were better than the old ones because there was not so much wood to catch fire and burn down the town, as London had been burned down in the Great Fire in King Charles's reign, when he was a boy.

When she was sure that the grey sky was only the smoky fog of London, Barbara got down. A smell from inside the house reached her. Coffee! Aunt Anne was making coffee, and coffee in the morning was the rarest of treats. Usually she had a bowl of milk or a dish of whey, while Geoffrey drank small ale with Father. Sometimes there was a pot of chocolate. But coffee! Certainly to-day must be a very special day.

Barbara's clothes

Barbara dressed herself. The clothes she was to wear had been hung out on a chair the night before when all the baggage was packed. The bodice was boned and hard to lace, and the skirt stood out stiffly. She preferred old dresses which were soft and could be hitched up when she played, but to-day she was ready to put up with anything. Quickly she brushed her curls and ran across the passage to Geoffrey's room. Geoffrey was her brother, two years older than herself, a schoolboy at Westminster School. He had been ill and Father was afraid that he might take the smallpox and die, as Mother had died last year. In fact it was because of Geoffrey's illness that he was taking them both with him to the country.

They were going further than Barbara had ever been before, to a place called Ladybourne. Aunt Anne said it was by the river Thames, near Henley, and almost half-way to Oxford. They would have to cross Hounslow Heath, and Barbara dreaded that part. There were footpads on Hounslow Heath. Nell, the serving maid, had bloodcurdling stories to tell about footpads. Travellers had been attacked and robbed, and even left tied to trees, according to Nell. Though Aunt Anne scolded her for telling such tales, they had a fascination for Barbara and she could never resist asking Nell for more. But it was one thing to listen to stories about footpads when one was safe and warm beside the kitchen fire, and quite another to think of them when one was going to cross Hounslow Heath. Barbara was thankful to remember that she would be on Father's horse, with Father's broad back in front of her, and her two arms clinging to Father's waist.

At Ladybourne they were going to stay at the inn, for Father had work to do. He was going to build a house. A Great House, Ladybourne Hall, stood there already, in a park near the river. But it was a very old-fashioned house, and, as the owner was going to be married, he wanted it pulled down and a fine new mansion built in its place. It would be the most important work that Father had ever done, and take months, or even years, to complete. So it had been decided that they should go and stay at the Wheatsheaf at Ladybourne. Father had made arrangements for Mrs. Jarvis, the innkeeper's wife, to look after the children. She was a kind, motherly soul, and with good country food and fresh air, Geoffrey would grow strong again.

He was still asleep when Barbara opened the door, the curtains of his bed half drawn against the night air. His face

3

looked thin and white, and his hair was much shorter than was the fashion. It had been cropped during his illness and had not yet grown long again. She stood uncertain whether to disturb him, but as she hesitated he woke, rubbed his eyes, and asked what o'clock it was.

Barbara made a guess, for the milkmaids usually called about seven. Then she told him the joyful news about the coffee and left him to dress.

She ran downstairs, pausing to hang over the balusters and sniff. Below she could hear the dry rattle of the pump handle and Aunt Anne's voice chiding Nell because no water came. Once again she had missed the time when it could be drawn. Silly wench, how often had it been explained to her that the watermills only supplied water to the pipes at certain hours of the day. And yet, instead of pumping then to fill the cistern, she must needs wait till they were dry. What was the good of the master having water laid on if she was too lazy to use it. Now she would please take her bucket and go out to the public conduit. If she had to wait her turn to get to the tank, she had only herself to blame.

Barbara almost laughed. Every day Nell forgot to draw the water at the proper time, and every day Aunt Anne scolded her. But no one took any notice of Aunt Anne's scoldings. They were like summer clouds. The sun was just behind them. The only reason she felt a little sorry about going away was because of Aunt Anne, who was Father's sister, and had lived with them ever since Mother died. Even in the country she would miss Aunt Anne.

At that moment, Father heard her on the stairs and called her into the parlour. Hoping she had done nothing wrong, Barbara pushed open the heavy door, and made her curtsey. Father too was dressed for a special day. He wore his best periwig, just back from being curled, and his new cloth riding coat was cut in the latest fashion with the pockets set low in the skirts.

But though he looked so frighteningly modish, Father was in a fine good humour. He called her his Poppet, and swung her right up into the air, big girl as she was. He had some good news for her, he said. She could have three guesses.

Barbara made the first guess at once. Was Aunt Anne coming with them to Ladybourne?

4

Father swung Barbara into the air

Father shook his head. He was sorry. Aunt Anne must remain in London because he might have to come back sometimes to see to his other work, and then what would he do if there were no one left to look after him? Guess again.

Barbara wrinkled her brow. If it was very good news it must be that they were never coming back to London at all, but she did not like to say that. It might sound unkind. She was still puzzling when Geoffrey came in. He got the answer right first time. They were going to travel by river.

Barbara gave a gasp of joy and Father laughed at her excitement. He'd engaged a boat with two rowing men, he said, and they would go up with the tide as far as Isleworth. The horses would await them there. It would be much better than riding through the crowded London streets, and anyway he wanted Geoffrey to see the new hospital at Chelsea which Sir Christopher Wren had just built for the King. (Father still said 'the King' when he meant King Charles, although King Charles had been dead five years, King James had come and gone, and now there was the Dutch King William and Queen Mary.) Geoffrey was delighted. He had already decided that he wanted to be an architect too, and he was very proud when Father took him round to show him fine buildings, and consult with him about the new houses he had planned.

Aunt Anne came in bearing the coffee-pot, followed by Nell with a tray on which was a pasty and a tankard of small ale for Father, a pile of oatcakes, and a dish of butter for the children. She had a piece of news to add to Father's. She was coming with them in the boat to Isleworth. They would sleep the night there at the inn, and the next morning when they set off on horseback, she would come back by coach to London.

Barbara heaved a sigh of satisfaction and turned her attention to her bowl of coffee. It was delicious, and the oatcakes were crisp and fresh. Certainly the day had begun very well.

Tankard, coffee-pot and porringers

London River from Essex Stairs

Chapter Two

THEY were still sitting at the table when Nell came to say that the porter was at the door. The heavy luggage was to go by road with the carrier plying between Henley and London, who would deliver it direct to the Wheatsheaf at Ladybourne. It might take two or three days to get there, but as they were taking with them in cloak bags the few things necessary for a couple of nights, that would not matter at all.

Father went off with Geoffrey at his heels. Barbara wanted to go too, but Aunt Anne told her to sit still and finish her coffee. There was nothing to see. The porters would simply take the trunks to the Three Tuns tavern by Charing Cross and put them on the carrier's wagon. Better stay quiet until it was time to get ready. And anyway she had something to give her.

'Something' proved to be a purse—a gay little purse of blue woven silk which Aunt Anne had made with her own hands, smaller copy of one she had made for Father. Barbara's was gathered up on to blue riband, long enough for it to dangle and swing, and, most thrilling of all, it was heavy with money.

Barbara's fingers were shaking so that she could hardly open it flat upon the table.

7

Inside was a little pile of coins—a farthing, a halfpenny, a silver penny and a silver groat, which was worth four pennies, a shilling, a half-crown, a great heavy crown piece, and, best of all, a real golden guinea.

Aunt Anne smiled at her excitement. She had given her one of every coin in circulation, she said. It would teach her the value of money. Now that she was going away from home, it was good for her to have some of her own. But she must take care of it and not spend it all at once. And she should tie it securely to her waist. There were so many cutpurses in the streets lately. In fact, when she was travelling, it would be a good idea to tuck it inside her bodice. The strings were long enough for that.

The word cutpurse reminded Barbara of Nell's stories, and her heart missed a beat as she realized that she was now worth

Patten and galoshe

robbing. But while she hesitated about confiding in Aunt Anne, Geoffrey came running to say that Father thought they should start soon if they were to reach Isleworth on the flow of the tide.

For the next few minutes everything was stir and bustle. Barbara wore her blue hooded cloak and carried her own bag containing her night smock and brush and comb. Aunt Anne insisted that she should put on her pattens, because the streets were muddy. Barbara hated pattens. They were thick wooden soles which were strapped on to her shoes, and they were hard and uncomfortable. But Aunt Anne told her not to make a fuss. Wooden pattens were not half as heavy as the iron galoshes that *she* was going to wear. And anyway they could be taken off in the boat.

At last everybody was ready, and with Nell standing at the door to see them go, they left the house and turned down towards the Strand.

The grey morning had broken into bright spring sunshine and a light breeze rocked the signboards over the shop doors, making a shifting pattern of shadows on the cobbles. There was no room on the footpath for them all to walk together, for the gutters were, as usual, transformed into rivers by the slop buckets of the housewives. So Father and Geoffrey led the way, with Aunt Anne and Barbara close behind them.

Geoffrey was completely happy. To walk through London with Father was his idea of perfect enjoyment, stopping to look at this house or that, noticing what bricks had been used and how they were laid, criticizing the pitch of the roof or the arrangement of the windows. Father was always ready to discuss problems of building with him, for he regarded it as part of Geoffrey's education. The boy had already picked up an astonishing amount of practical knowledge. For, though it was agreed that Geoffrey was to be an architect, it was still undecided how he was to become one. Geoffrey had set his heart on going to Oxford as Sir Christopher had done—Sir Christopher was Geoffrey's hero—but Father insisted that Oxford was not necessary. Instead Geoffrey could be apprenticed to a master builder when he left school, and learn his business that way. Geoffrey sometimes tried to argue about it, but he never got very far, for Father was not the sort of person to be argued with, and only Barbara knew how much he really longed for Oxford.

The Strand was full of mud, and of coaches and drays and wagons churning backwards and forwards between London and Westminster. Aunt Anne said that the traffic was dreadfully dangerous, far worse than it used to be when she was a girl. In those days everyone travelled by river when they wanted to get from one end of the town to the other. Nowadays half of them went by road, rattling about in those hackney coaches from the stand over there by the Maypole. The drivers were a wild lot. Look! There was actually a fight going on between two of them at this moment.

She pointed along the Strand. Two hackney coaches, drawn across the road, blocked all the highway, while their coachmen slashed at one another with whips. Probably they both claimed the same fare, Father remarked scornfully. Nine times out of ten that was the trouble. Geoffrey wanted to go back and watch, but Father called to him to come along. They had no time to bother over street brawls, and he led the way down Essex Street. Essex Street was his favourite route to the river. He had drawn the plans for some of the new houses which were just finished, and he and Geoffrey always stopped to look at them. Barbara secretly thought they were hideous, with their flat fronts of bright red brick and their neat sash windows. But she liked going under the watergate of the old Essex House which still stood at the bottom of the street. She ran through the gate ahead of the others and waited, looking around her.

The river lay in a wide silver sweep, its near bank littered by a jumble of sheds and warehouses put up hastily upon the derelict foreshore of old Essex House. But over the sheds the sun shone upon the distant scaffolding of the half-built St. Paul's, upon the spires of bright new City churches, and, far away, upon buttresses and arches of old London Bridge with the untidy jumble of houses built upon it.

The tide was low. At the bottom of Essex Stairs a stretch of mud, bridged by a gangway of slippery planks, lay between the steps and the boats. A group of watermen, waiting at the river's edge, all broke at once into shouts and catcalls as Father and Aunt Anne appeared through the arch. Each boatman claimed that it was his boat they had engaged. One man in particular, a burly figure with a tousled mop of red hair and a black patch over the left eye, yelled more persistently than the others. But Father shook his head and pointed to a boat drawn to the end of the footway, where two rowing men were already preparing to cast off.

Geoffrey was first down the stairs and along the plank. He clambered into the boat, and called back to Barbara, telling her to hurry up. It was not nearly so slippery if one took it quickly.

But Barbara just didn't dare to hurry. Her wooden pattens slid and slithered on the slimy boards. Once she lost her balance and would have landed in the mud if a pair of great dirty hands had not reached out and grasped her. She glanced up and saw to her dismay that the hands belonged to the horrible rough man with the black patch. She struggled to free herself, but there was nothing else to hold on to and she was forced to cling to him. To make matters worse the blue purse jolted out of her bodice and jingled between them, swinging by its riband. The man laughed and made a playful grab at it, but Barbara snatched it back, and dodging free of him, plunged for the boat. Geoffrey dragged her in, and she sank down, shaken and frightened, on the back seat.

By the time that Father and Aunt Anne had picked their way across the gangway she had recovered. Geoffrey called to her to look down the river. He wanted to describe how he had shot the rapids under London Bridge the day he went down to Greenwich with Father. Barbara had heard the story often before, but she let him run on. She had plenty to look at, for the river was seething with life. There were dignified Tilt boats with four or five men rowing and an awning over the little crowd of passengers. There was a public barge starting on its daily journey up to Windsor. There were heavy flat-

Boats on London River

bottomed sailing barges carrying sea-coal, and little wherries, like the one they were sitting in, with a couple of rowing men. And there were dozens of small boats moving in every direction like flies on a ceiling, with watermen yelling and shouting to avoid collision and pulling at their sculls as if they were rowing for a wager instead of carrying sober passengers who had paid money to be taken safely to their destination.

As soon as Father and Aunt Anne were settled the oarsmen pushed out into deep water. They were speeded on their way by a chorus from the rest of the gang—the man with the black patch standing up in his boat to bawl the louder. Barbara was thankful to leave him behind. As the wherry gained headway she settled down beside Aunt Anne. At last they had really started on the journey to Ladybourne.

The river bank was full of interest and Father did not let

them miss anything. First they passed the fine mansions of the Strand, each with its gardens, its cluster of outbuildings, its watergate and its private stairs—Somerset House, The Savoy, Northumberland House. Others had recently been pulled down and new streets built in their place, and Father called repeatedly to Geoffrey to notice a row of houses here or a church tower there. After the great mansions came the palace of Whitehall, like a little town in itself, with the covered stairs for the King to enter the royal barge. Soon they reached Westminster and the watermen rested on their oars so that Barbara could see Parliament Stairs and the Chamber of Parliament close to the river, with the long roof of Westminster Hall behind it and behind again the pinnacles of the Abbey, and the buildings of Geoffrey's school.

Westminster passed Father relaxed, for the town was dissolving into country, the sun shone high overhead, and it was very hot. Barbara had already dropped her cloak. Father and Geoffrey each took off their coats and sat in shirts and ruffles. Father's face was red under his great periwig, and Barbara thought that he must envy the watermen who wore their own hair cropped short, very much as Geoffrey wore his. Geoffrey had made a great fuss when he found that his long hair had been cut off in his illness, and he had begged Father to let him have a periwig. But Father had refused. Though he wore fine clothes himself, and fell in with the way of the fashionable world because it helped his career to do so, Father came of Puritan stock, and was strict in the upbringing of his children. No fairs, no cock-fighting or bull-baiting, no theatres; plain clothes and sober living; those were his principles. As for Geoffrey's periwig, it would be time enough when he reached the sixth form at Westminster. Looking at Father's hot face Barbara reflected that at this moment Geoffrey must be feeling rather glad.

She dangled her fingers in the water to cool them and felt envious of some boys who were bathing from the Mill bank. On the other side of the river, near Vauxhall Gardens, a party of fashionable ladies and fine gentlemen rested in the shade of a tree. They had brought musical instruments to amuse themselves and one lady plucked the strings of a lute while a gentleman piped upon a flageolet. Barbara turned to watch them. She loved a flageolet, with its high flute-like notes. Geoffrey had one, and she far preferred picking out tunes to practising on the virginals which Aunt Anne taught her. The silvery music carried over the water and followed them long after they had swung round the next bend and left Vauxhall behind them.

Barbara was beginning to feel hungry. It was only a little way to Chelsea, Aunt Anne consoled her. At Chelsea Stairs they would land and have their dinner at the tavern. They were just coming now to the new Chelsea Hospital which Father wanted them to see. Already he was directing the watermen to pull away to the other side of the river, so that they could take in the whole line of it, built on rising ground and crowned with a tiny copper dome which sparkled in the sunlight.

Geoffrey stood up to gaze at the work of his beloved Sir Christopher, and Father discoursed lengthily upon its beauties.

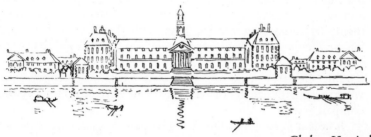

Chelsea Hospital

Barbara remained suitably silent, and presently became more interested in the mallards moving among the reeds of Battersea marshes, just behind them. One mother duck actually had half a dozen fluffy babies which she was vainly trying to coax back into shelter, and Barbara excitedly pulled at Aunt Anne's sleeve. Battersea marshes were a grand place for wild fowl, one of the boatmen told her. Of course it was all preserved. No one was allowed to shoot or trap it. But all the same, plenty of cottages in Chelsea had a roasted wild duck now and again, and no questions asked.

While she peered into the tangled backwater, she heard the creak of rowlocks behind them. A small boat was pulling up the river with one man at the oars. He was singing to himself as he pulled—'Lillibullero'—the tune that everyone was whist-ling. The gruff hearty voice made Barbara look round. To her disgust she recognized Black Patch. She had been so thankful to leave him behind at Essex Stairs. What was he doing here? It looked almost as if he were following them.

But the little boat was moving fast, and it was already far ahead when Father turned away from Chelsea Hospital and gave orders to row on. They had only a very little way to go before they reached Chelsea village, by the church.

The tavern was crowded. But the landlord led them to a room upstairs where he promised that the ordinary should be served at once.

Barbara sat waiting with Geoffrey on the window-seat, looking out on the little quay. It was quite crowded. There were farm hands loading their produce on to barges to go to London. A coach drove up with two gentlemen waiting for the Tilt boat going downstream. A sedan chair delivered a lady passenger. A little girl with a basket was selling oranges and a group of watermen lounged at the top of the stairs. Among them Barbara recognized the man with the black patch. She felt suddenly frightened, and pulled at Geoffrey's sleeve to point the man out.

But Geoffrey was not interested. He was hungry, and watermen, with patches or without them, were of no importance compared with his dinner.

It was a very good dinner. The pewter plates were piping hot and the veal chops and gravy excellent. Forks were not laid, and Father insisted on calling for them. They might as well behave like modern civilized people while they could, he observed—though probably they would get no forks at the Wheatsheaf.

Back in the wherry everybody was quiet. The only excitement of the afternoon was the passage downstream of a raft of great tree trunks lashed together. They were kept on their course by watermen in a barge on one side, and, on the other, by men with long poles running along the bank. Seasoned oak, Father re-

Spoon, fork and knife

14

marked; floating down to the dockyards to build ships for the Navy.

At Chiswick they stopped again at a coffee-house. Barbara was very tired. The seat was hard and she had pins and needles. The sun sank behind trees. Every time they came to a village she hoped that it was Isleworth but still the watermen rowed on. Leaning against Aunt Anne's shoulder, she slept.

The jolting of the boat as it touched the bank woke her. At last they had arrived.

There was a quay and a flight of steps. But thanks to the high tide, there was not much climbing to be done. Geoffrey jumped ashore and Barbara stretched her arm for him to pull her up too.

But instead of Geoffrey's, a big hairy hand gripped hers. As she scrambled on to the wharf she recognized it. It was Black Patch once more.

He helped her quite gently, and Barbara controlled herself enough to thank him. He grinned at her. But when he grinned he looked worse than ever, for he showed a mouth of broken and discoloured fangs. As Barbara struggled to conceal her shudder, he told her that the sun had set for stormy weather, and added mysteriously that maybe he'd see them again before long.

See them again? What on earth could he mean? Why was he following them like this? She went cold at the thought, and walking up the yard to the inn, she clung desperately to Aunt Anne.

Looking down at her white face, Aunt Anne wanted to know what was the matter. Poor child, she was so tired. She was trembling. Was anything wrong? Had something frightened her?

Barbara was incoherent. That dreadful man had followed them all the way from Essex Stairs, she cried. He wanted to rob them. She'd only just saved her purse from him this morning. He'd be waiting for them on Hounslow Heath to-morrow.

The more Aunt Anne soothed her, the worse it seemed to be. At last Father came to inquire what the trouble was about.

He frowned a little as he listened to her story. If the man really had tried to snatch her purse, it was odd that he should be following them. Barbara must not worry. While supper was preparing, he would go and see what he could find out.

15

With warm water to wash her face and hands, Barbara grew calm again. When Father returned he was smiling.

Well, she hadn't caught a highwayman this time, he teased her. The man was just an ordinary waterman, going to Windsor to join the crew of a barge with sea-coal for Oxford. He seemed a good-natured fellow. His name was Sam Pullet. All these watermen knew one another, so he'd heard about their journey. He knew Ladybourne well—passed it every time he took his barge up the river. That was why he'd joked that he'd see them again. As for her purse, he said that he had saved it from falling in the mud. Was she satisfied now?

Barbara was. She felt a little ashamed of having made such a fuss. But all the same she hated Sam Pullet, with his black patch and his horrible teeth. She cordially hoped that she would *not* see him at Ladybourne.

The inn was warm and comfortable. The host hovered round to see they had all they wanted, and after supper he with his fiddle and his wife at the virginals played music for their entertainment.

But Barbara longed only for bed, and Aunt Anne told her to say Good night. The bed was an old-fashioned one, panelled and roofed. Barbara tucked her purse under her pillow. As she drifted into sleep, the sound of the fiddle grew fainter and fainter, till it was lost in the rhythm of splashing oars.

Flageolet and lute

16

Traffic on the road

Chapter Three

BARBARA was up early in the morning, and while Aunt Anne re-packed their night clothes, she went out to join Father and Geoffrey on the quay. They were watching strings of big barges, their sails very red in the morning sun, slipping away down to London on the ebb tide.

They were sea-going barges, Father told them. Probably they'd brought coal round the coast from Newcastle. It was called sea-coal because it was carried by sea. They would take it up as far as Staines or Windsor. There it would be loaded on to other barges—smaller ones for the river—and carried to all the inland towns. That was what Barbara's friend, Sam Pullet, was going to do.

Barbara flushed. She was trying to forget about Sam Pullet and her stupidity yesterday, and she was glad when the host came to say that breakfast was on the table.

Aunt Anne was to leave them directly after breakfast. She was going to visit a friend near-by in Brentford, and a coach was coming to fetch her. She was a little bit anxious and full of last-minute instructions to Barbara. Barbara must see that Geoffrey wore his quilted waistcoat if it turned cold. And let her not forget to use her own new toothbrush from France. It was not every little girl who had a toothbrush. If she liked she might add a little honey to her mouth-wash of vinegar and cinnamon. But above all she must remember to wear her

Barbara said good-bye to Aunt Anne

hare's foot charm if there was any smallpox about, and take care that Geoffrey wore his.

Barbara promised everything she asked. She was just beginning to realize how much she would miss Aunt Anne, and at breakfast only Father and Geoffrey really did justice to the cold meat, the pasties and cheese and the tankards of ale with which the table was loaded. As it was they had barely finished when the coach from Brentford arrived.

It was soon over. Barbara clung tightly to Aunt Anne as she said good-bye. The coachman settled on his seat. The leathers creaked and the coach trundled noisily away. There was no time to fret, for already the ostler had brought the horses out into the yard. Silver, Father's own big grey, was an old friend of Barbara's. And there was a little bay mare hired for Geoffrey. The riding things had come down in the wherry yesterday — Father's high boots beeswaxed till they shone like glass, Father's own saddle and saddlecloth, his cloak and pistol and holster.

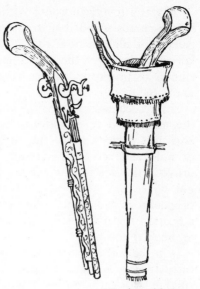

Pistols and holster

Geoffrey had the pistol half out of its case when Father appeared in the doorway and called sharply to him to put it back. Firearms were not toys to be trifled with. He'd do better to look sharp and get into his boots. It was high time for them to start.

Barbara, already in her cloak, watched the ostler fasten her pillion seat behind Father's saddle. It was the first time she had ridden pillion. On the last long ride she was quite a little girl and travelled perched in front of Father. She had to wait while Father mounted. Then the ostler put her up, helped her to settle and showed her how to hold on. Geoffrey came running back, and flung himself into his saddle as if his mount were a fiery and mettlesome steed rather than a peaceful hack from the posting-house.

At last they were off, picking their way through the cobbled streets of Isleworth, walking their horses until they left the houses behind them and turned on to the short grass that fringed the dreaded Hounslow Heath.

With Father's broad back before her Barbara forgot to worry about footpads and highwaymen, and after feeling to make sure that her precious purse was safely tucked into her bodice she settled down to enjoy herself.

19

It was a lovely morning with a fresh breeze from the west. Fleecy clouds scudded in front of the sun. They threw little patches of blue shadow that raced across the grass, flitted like fairy curtains over the copses and played hide and seek with clumps of primroses on the banks and the carpets of bluebells under the trees.

Father seemed to know the way very well. He would avoid the main road to Brentford, he said. At this time of year, after the winter's rains, the roads were bad—just a quagmire of mud and ruts. As a result, in open country, each coach drove at the side to avoid the tracks of the last one till the road got wider and wider and it was impossible to tell where the original road had been. The churned-up ground was sometimes a quarter of a mile wide. He meant to keep to the open Heath as much as possible.

On the soft turf the horses' hoofs made no noise and sound carried far. Barbara became aware of the song of birds, ringing as clearly as the flagcolet over the river yesterday. Of course there were birds in London, but one never noticed them amid the noises of the City. Here they dominated everything. She hung her head right back, trying to see a lark which soared above them and trilled notes as clear and clean as the washed blue and white of the sky.

Suddenly Father reined his horse. It was so unexpected that Barbara almost fell backwards. He called a warning to Geoffrey, and she felt his hand slide towards his pistol holster. From behind a thicket to their left galloped three horsemen, one ahead, and two in pursuit. Barbara's heart leapt into her throat. For a moment the hoofs thundered along the turf just beside them. Silver curvetted nervously under Father's restraining hand. But the horsemen were intent only upon their own affairs. They swept in a wide curve ahead, and the leading man left the track again, hotly followed by the other two. Their heads were visible, here and there above the bushes in the distance, long after the drumming of hoofs had died away.

Father relaxed and moved forward once more, as Geoffrey and Barbara overwhelmed him with questions. Were they highwaymen? Was the man in front going to be robbed? Would he get away? Could they go after them and find out?

But Father could not satisfy their curiosity. It might have been two honest men after one rascal, or two rascals after one honest man. Or it might have been just a private quarrel. It was impossible to tell. But as for going after them, the solitary man had not called for help, and it was none of their business.

Barbara shivered a little and pressed closer to Father. It seemed as though the world had changed suddenly. The Heath was no longer a lovely place of spring flowers and bird song. There was ugliness in it. Even the sun had vanished behind a cloud. As they crested a low hillock the first spot of rain fell.

In a dip just ahead lay the road. As Father had described, it was just a broad stretch of mud. Traffic moved in both directions, but it was widely scattered, each traveller trying to find the firmest ground. A carrier's wagon with six great horses lurched and trundled slowly towards London, two carters on foot beside it squelching through the mud, and the heads of passengers peering from under the hood at the back. A string of packhorses skirted the edge of the track, and three men on horseback picked their way single file along the centre.

Further ahead a little knot of people was collected round a tilted coach, where men with crowbars heaved and horses struggled. Bogged in the mud, said Father. Poor people, they might be stuck there for hours. Luckily they were not too far from civilization. When that happened at remote places on the roads, passengers sometimes had to spend the night in their coaches.

Barbara peeped in as they passed and saw that the occupants were an old lady with white hair under a velvet hood, and a gentleman in the black clothes and white bands of a clergyman.

Were all the highways like this one? Geoffrey inquired. Didn't someone have to look after them? If the Romans had good roads all those hundreds of years ago, why were they so bad now?

Father glanced over his shoulder to see that Barbara had her cloak, for the rain was coming on fast.

They weren't all as bad as this, he explained. In fact, some parts were quite well kept, with clean ditches and trimmed hedges. It all depended on the parishes that the road passed through, for every parish was responsible for its own bit of highway. The people had to pay for it or mend it with their own hands. Some were good about it and some were lazy. You couldn't really blame them. It was hard lines on a country village if their road was churned up by coaches of rich people

21

going to Bath, for instance. They might well be angry if they had to give up their farm work to do repairs, without receiving a penny piece in payment. There had been several attempts to charge coaches with a toll, but it had never succeeded. Anyway there were not many places where there was so much traffic as this road to London across Hounslow Heath.

By now the rain was coming down in torrents. Father spread his riding cloak like a tent right over Barbara. She was quite dry under it, but it was stuffy and airless. She leaned her head against his back and dozed. How long she slept she did not know, but a change in the movement of the horse woke her. Father raised the cloak and warned her to sit quite still. He must dismount. Silver was lame. He thought it was a cast shoe.

The sudden light made Barbara blink. They were standing by the side of the road in country so flat that it was completely blotted out by sheets of rain. Geoffrey on his hack was streaming with water which poured from the sodden brim of his beaver. Father looked up from his examination of the horse's forefoot, his periwig lank and dripping. Silver had cast a shoe some way back and could not go on with a double load. Barbara must stay where she was and he would walk at the bridle until they reached a smithy. Luckily it was not far to Colnbrook.

Wrapped in Father's cloak she sat alone on Silver's back. She pulled her hood right over her face but the rain ran down her neck and found its way into every crevice. So the damp little procession trailed on till they clattered on the cobblestones of Colnbrook.

Outside the blacksmith's Father flung Silver's rein over a hook, and lifted Barbara down. She could go into the forge, he said, and dry herself by the fire while Silver was being shod.

The forge seemed pitch dark except for the red glow of the open fire. The smith himself, a huge man girded in a leather apron, handled a red-hot shoe from the embers with a pair of tongs and hammered it upon the anvil until the sparks flew. A boy, crouching beside the fire, fanned the flame with bellows.

Barbara and Geoffrey both stood by the hearth watching him. Under her cloak Barbara was not really wet, but from Geoffrey's clothes the steam began to rise. He did not seem to worry. He was too intent on looking around him. The way that things were made always fascinated Geoffrey, and he called Barbara's attention to the metal work lying about everywhere: plough-shares, spades and sickles, domestic pots and pans all waiting to be mended. A lead cistern took a lot of space. Behind it stood a new fire-back, embossed with the date, 1690, and beyond that

Blacksmith's shop

again, half lost in shadows, a pair of wrought-iron gates.

Geoffrey said aloud that he would rather like to be a smith, and then grinned as Barbara laughed at him. It was a standing joke that Geoffrey, when he was small, had wanted to be so many different things—a postilion, an apothecary, an artist— for ages he had wanted to be an artist, and he still spent most of his spare time drawing or painting. But that was before he had decided for certain that he would be an architect.

A pungent acrid smell, as the smith got to work on the hoof, made Barbara wish that she had something to sniff—Aunt Anne's pomander, or the orange stuck with cloves which she used when London smells were worse than usual.

Just then there was a rumble of wheels and the doorway of the forge was darkened by the shadow of a coach. A man's voice called loudly for the smith. Geoffrey and Barbara peeped to see what was happening.

Outside stood the very coach which had been stuck in the mud miles back. Barbara recognized the clergyman and the old lady in the velvet hood. They were both peering anxiously through the glass. Apparently it was the matter of an axle pin strained in getting the wheel out of the mud. Grumbling that it was really a job for the wheelwright, the smith took a great hammer and dealt the hub one or two resounding blows. Barbara stuffed her fingers in her ears, noticing as she did so that the lady had beckoned to Father, who stepped up to the coach to talk to her. After a few moments he turned and called Barbara. Wondering, Barbara obeyed.

This kind lady, Father explained, was concerned to see a little girl riding pillion in such weather. The coach was going to Reading and she had offered to take Barbara as far as Maidenhead. They would wait at the Bear Inn, and Father and Geoffrey would pick her up there.

In vain Barbara protested that she did not mind the rain and would rather ride. She found herself bundled inside the coach, and the door closed upon her.

Her host and hostess were kindness itself. The lady insisted on taking her damp cloak and wrapping her in a shawl while the clergyman produced some gingerbread. Barbara dis-

The Brooksbanks' new coach

covered that she was hungry, and the sweetmeat cured her shyness. In a few minutes she was chattering freely, answering the lady's questions about Father and Geoffrey and herself and where they were going. The lady was very interested to hear that Father was an architect and a friend of Sir Christopher Wren, and when Barbara said that he was going to Ladybourne to rebuild the Great House there, she leaned forward to nod at her husband several times.

She knew Ladybourne very well, she said. Mrs. Hayward, the wife of the rector, was one of her oldest friends. She knew Sir Humphrey Ainsley too, for whom Father was going to build this grand new house. He was going to marry an heiress, so of course the old Hall was not fine enough for *her*. Did Barbara know that he was a widower and had a little daughter by his first marriage? Elizabeth was her name. Old Lady Ainsley was bringing her up. Perhaps Barbara would be allowed to play with her. Anyway, she would get to know Parson Hayward and his wife. She must be sure to tell Mrs. Hayward that she had ridden with Mrs. Brooksbank, in her new coach— Parson Brooksbank, she had better say: the Reverend Abraham Brooksbank of St. Mary's Church in Reading. But she must be sure to mention the coach—and the glass windows—particularly the glass windows.

Barbara said Yes politely, but her attention was wandering. Parson Brooksbank had produced his watch, and it chimed the hour—three little silvery notes for three o'clock, and then three more quickly for the quarters, to show that it was a quarter before four, he explained. Barbara had never seen a watch like that—a repeater, he called it. It was a new and wonderful invention. He let her hold it in her hand, a heavy watch, smooth and round, of beautiful chased and enamelled silver. Barbara wished that she could show it to Geoffrey.

All this while the coach lumbered on, swinging quite smoothly at first, then lurching and bumping as they came to a bad bit of road. Barbara almost preferred the bumps to the swinging motion. Parson Brooksbank explained that it was caused by the long leather straps on which the body was slung. It was the very latest mode in coach building, and as sweet and easy as a boat riding at anchor. Barbara thought that he had described it exactly. It swung just like a boat. She began to feel sick, and wished she were back on the horse again, rain or no rain. Mrs. Brooksbank cleared a patch on the steamy glass and said that it was not far to Maidenhead. They had just passed the Bell and Crown Inn at Taplow. Soon they would cross the river. The Bear, where they were to wait for Father, lay on the other side.

They halted just short of the river, and Parson Brooksbank opened the door. A wagon was crossing Maidenhead Bridge, he said. It was only a narrow bridge built on piles and there was no room for two vehicles to pass. It had stopped raining Barbara could jump out for a breath of air if she liked.

Barbara did like. She stood beside the coach, drinking in great gulps of fresh air. Everything was grey, and the river swirled in a sullen torrent against the wooden posts of the bridge. It was difficult to realize that this was the same river on which they had rowed so easily yesterday. But the wind carried a fresh smell of leaves and blossom and wet earth, and she got back into the coach not caring how soaked her feet might be.

The Bear, a great posting-house, was much bigger than the inn at Isleworth, and it was full of people coming and going. The particular bustle to-day, so Parson Brooksbank informed them, was due to the coaches and horses of the judges and lawyers, on their way to hold their assize courts in the county towns. Nowadays everyone had taken to gadding about—— Why, actually the flying coaches went from Oxford to London in a single day and the fare was only about threepence a mile. No wonder the roads were getting more crowded every year.

He led the way into the hall of the inn, where a log fire crackled, and travellers rested their pewter tankards upon a great bulbous-legged oak table. Mulled ale, he said, would save them from an ague, and Mrs. Brooksbank and Barbara waited on a tall settle while he ordered it. Almost immediately, greatly to Barbara's relief, Father and Geoffrey arrived to join them. The weather was clearing, they declared. They had ridden from Colnbrook almost without a drop of rain.

Barbara begged Parson Brooksbank to show Geoffrey his watch. Geoffrey was thrilled, as she had known he would be. Of course he wanted to see how it was made and why it repeated the hour like that, and he pored over it with the parson, and with Father too, until the mulled ale arrived.

From that moment Barbara noticed little more. The ale was warm and sweet, and as she sipped it she grew so sleepy that she did not see the Brooksbanks go. She did not even remember being wrapped in her cloak and laid across the front of Father's saddle. When she woke up she was lulled and comfortable with her head against his shoulder. The horses were threading their way among woods down a long hill. Though it was almost dark, a full moon was rising through the trees. Presently they passed some cottages, thatched and whitewashed, with the yellow glimmer of candlelight in the tiny windows. The road broadened in front of a pair of tall wrought-iron gates. Father broke his silence to draw Geoffrey's attention to the entrance to Ladybourne Hall.

Just a little further and they turned aside and stopped before a thatched house. A signboard swung, gently creaking, on a bracket.

This was the Wheatsheaf Inn.

26

'The Wheatsheaf'

Chapter Four

AS they halted, the door opened and a man came out, followed by a woman, a plump and comfortable figure against the lighted doorway.

Father greeted them warmly. He called the woman to come near. He had a tired little girl to give to her. Barbara felt herself lifted and laid in motherly arms. This, then, must be Mrs. Jarvis.

The kitchen into which she was taken was a low room with a beamed ceiling, a long table, and a blazing fire in the great chimney place. Mrs. Jarvis sat her in the inglenook and drew her shoes from her feet. Father, with Geoffrey, came in after them. How warm and cheerful it looked, he exclaimed. They would certainly have supper here by the fire, rather than in the parlour.

Mrs. Jarvis bustled round, piling the table with good things, a pair of capons, a great ham, a leg of mutton, wooden bowls of steaming soup and wooden platters of country clap bread, while her husband hurried in from the taproom with tankards of cider.

Barbara, in her chimney corner, with a bowl of bread and milk, was almost too tired to eat. She sat playing with her spoon and listening, half in a dream, to the talk at the table, and to the unfamiliar sounds which came through the open door from the taproom beyond—the jangle of drinking cans, the

27

click of wooden balls among the ninepins, and the drawl of broad country voices.

At last Father told her that she had best go to bed. Mrs. Jarvis opened a door in the wall and led the way up tiny twisting stairs. At the top a candle glowed in a little white room under the thatched roof. The truckle bed in the corner was already turned down. Its snowy sheets and patchwork coverlet looked inviting.

As she snuggled into the soft depths, Barbara gave a deep sigh of content. Though it was all new and the people around her were strangers, she felt that she had come home.

The oak coffer with ewer and bowl

When she woke in the morning she could not at first remember where she was. She had burrowed a hole for herself in the feather mattress, and she could see nothing but the rough plaster ceiling which lined the thatch and sloped to within a few inches of her head.

Gradually all that had happened yesterday came back to her. She did not uncurl till she had got it clearly. But even then it did not seem real until she heard Mrs. Jarvis's voice downstairs calling to someone to bring those buckets from the well and look sharp about it.

Barbara sat up. Sunshine poured through the leaded panes and drew a diamond pattern on the floor. There was hardly any furniture; a plain oak coffer, a wooden stool and a mat of plaited rushes. In the corner the angle of the thatch was boarded to form a cupboard. A pitcher and bowl for washing stood on the coffer; a tiny mirror hung on the wall. But it was spotlessly clean and the sheets smelled of lavender.

When she opened the tiny casement and put out her head, she got a shock. The sun was high in the heavens. Father and Geoffrey, both fully dressed, stood on the cobbles below talking to a strange man. She dodged in again before they could see her, and peeped at them from the side. He was a tall spare man. He wore a cloth coat of a dull smoky grey, and under a high-crowned hat his hair, uncurled, hung in a mode which was long out of date in London.

Barbara slipped into her clothes and went downstairs.

At the kitchen table Mrs. Jarvis was making pastry. She asked Barbara how she had slept, and then laughed at herself. She need not have asked. It was nearly noon, and the men would soon be coming in for their dinner. Did Miss Barbara want a morning draught? There was milk in the dairy, or a bowl of curds if she liked it.

But Barbara said she would rather wait for dinner. She would go and find Father.

He was outside, Mrs. Jarvis told her. She'd find them both in the yard talking to Mr. Lovegrove, my lady's bailiff. She thought that there was some troubling news, but she did not know. It was none of her business.

Barbara went outside. Seen in daylight the Wheatsheaf lay back sideways from the road. It was a rambling old house, much larger than it had looked at night. Its walls of oak beams and whitewashed plaster were broken by little windows with diamond panes, filled sometimes with horn, sometimes with lumpy distorted glass.

She crept up behind Father, careful to make no noise, for there was a rule in London that she must never intrude when he was in company.

Mr. Lovegrove, the bailiff, had a long nose in a bony face which looked as if it did not often smile. He turned a cold blue eye upon Barbara and said: 'Is this your daughter?' without changing the tone of his voice. Barbara made her curtsey, wishing that he had not noticed her.

But Father did not reply. He was looking worried, and

They were talking to the Bailiff

when, in a minute or two, he and the bailiff turned away together and walked back to the road, she whispered to Geoffrey to know what was the matter.

Geoffrey shook his head. It was bad news. They might have to go back to London.

Barbara gasped with horror. Back to London? Oh no! They *couldn't*. They had only just come. What had happened? Was it about the Great House?

'Hush!' said Geoffrey again, and raised his finger to his lips.

Mr. Lovegrove was departing. As he went he called back to Father that he would expect him at the Hall after dinner. Her ladyship and Miss Elizabeth had gone to Henley in the coach, so, if he wished, he might bring the children.

Mrs. Jarvis had laid their dinner in the parlour, on a gate-legged table spread with a white cloth. There were fresh rushes on the floor and a pitcher filled with bluebells on the table.

Father sat down and began to talk.

Sir Humphrey Ainsley was abroad, he said. He had been in Italy all the winter, and should have arrived home some weeks ago. But, as the children doubtless knew, we were at war with France, which meant that he could not get back by the direct route. He wrote from Rome to say that he must either await a ship, or travel a long way round. All this was a great delay when the plans were finished and they were waiting to begin the house. But to make matters worse, Lady Ainsley, Sir Humphrey's mother, had received news this morning that he was ill and still in Rome. He was not in danger of his life, but it might be some time before he was able to make that long journey.

Barbara looked at him blankly.

Then wouldn't he want the new house after all? she asked.

Her father reassured her. He would want it; that was certain. He was going to be married a second time, and his future wife desired a modern house. But nothing could be started until he came home. The old house had to be pulled down first, and his mother and his little daughter were still living in it. Now the great question was, were they to wait about and kick their heels in Ladybourne, until Sir Humphrey returned, or should they all just go back to London again?

To this question no one seemed to have an answer. There was a silence broken by Mrs. Jarvis and a young serving wench who carried in the dinner. Barbara and Geoffrey were hungry and attacked their food with zest. But Father had no appetite. While they ate, he began to talk again, going over and over the same problem. By the time that they had reached the cream and the sweetmeats, he had practically decided that it would be best for them all to go home, and come back again later on. There was a lot of work waiting for him in London. He could not afford to waste his time.

Barbara, looking through the open casement on to a sunny back-yard, felt desperate. Though she had only been here a few hours, already she loved the Wheatsheaf and everything about it. The yard was flanked by stacks of willow rods bleaching in the sun. Evidently they were intended for baskets like the ones which stood half-made on the bench outside the back door. She would love to make baskets. She would love to feed the chickens, and the little pink pigs which she could see scuttling about under the trees in the orchard. A new idea came into her mind, and despair made her bold.

She slipped from her stool and stood by Father's side, fingering his buttons nervously.

Couldn't she and Geoffrey stay here? she begged. He had told them already that he would have to go back to London sometimes, even after the house was begun. They would have to wait here for him then, so why couldn't they wait now, while he went back to do his other work? They would be quite safe with Mrs. Jarvis, and they would be *very* good.

Father laughed and pulled her ear. So she had fallen in love with Ladybourne, had she? Well, it was not a bad idea. He would think about it. Remember, he had not promised, but he certainly would consider it. Now, it was time that they got ready to go up to the Hall.

Barbara skipped off, feeling suddenly very cheerful. The day was hot but she could not change into a cooler dress because the carrier had not yet brought the luggage. Mrs. Jarvis said that three days was nothing for the wagon. If the roads were sticky the horses couldn't be expected to do much more than ten miles a day with all that load. However, she gave Barbara a pitcher of water from the well to wash her hands and face.

The tall wrought-iron gates of Ladybourne Hall stood open. Probably, Father said, the coach had just passed out, bearing her ladyship to Henley. It was fortunate that she had gone. That was why he was able to bring the children with him this afternoon. By Sir Humphrey's orders little Elizabeth was kept very strictly. Her mother had died of a sickness brought from outside, and he hated her to mix with strangers in case she caught something too. After all, that was easy to understand, wasn't it?

Geoffrey and Barbara readily agreed. The danger of infection was one that they had good reason to know, since their own mother had died of the smallpox.

An artist from London brought the sickness, Father told them—continuing the story as they walked up the drive. He came to paint young Lady Ainsley's portrait. She was a very beautiful woman. But the picture was never finished, for the artist, poor fellow, died too.

They walked on in solemn silence. It was a lovely afternoon. The sun glinted on the smooth silvery barks of the beeches, brilliant with young leaves. Rooks wheeled and called overhead. White sheep nibbled the fresh grass, and a little party of fallow deer moved shyly away among the trees.

Barbara was just about to remark that it seemed a long way

The gates of Ladybourne Hall

to the house, when they topped a ridge, and there it lay before them, nestling in a hollow.

There were so many buildings clustered together that, at first glance, Ladybourne Hall looked like a small village. It was largely self-supporting, Father explained. That was why it covered so much ground. It had its own farm and bakehouse and laundry and brewery, and what not else. In an old manor, such as this, these were not designed. They just grew up haphazard. So, when modern people wanted order and comfort, the best thing was to pull it all down and start afresh, as Sir Humphrey was going to do. To get the best view, they should come to the top of a little hill. From there they could see the house itself.

Geoffrey, with Barbara close behind, followed Father for a short distance up rising ground. Then they turned round.

Barbara drew a long breath. Looked at from up here, it was quite the loveliest house she had ever seen.

Geoffrey, gazing, observed at once the tremendous length of the roof tree. Its long single line, rising or sagging a little with age, stretched from end to end of the building. The tiles were a deep red, shading here and there to green or gold with moss or lichen. Gables and wings and chimneys grew from it as naturally as branches from a tree. Blue wood smoke, which rose transparent from tall chimney stacks, veiled part of the bank of trees beyond the house.

Father looked upon it with the eye of a student. It was an excellent example of its period, he said to Geoffrey. The earliest part, of course, was the great Hall, which occupied all the centre of that long roof tree. Those two parallel wings, which made it look rather like a letter H, were the chapel, and the library on one side, and the kitchens on the other. The rest of it grew, bit by bit, as people ceased to live herded together, and needed more room to breathe. It was certainly beautiful in its way, but of course it was entirely out of date. One could under-stand that the lady who was going to marry Sir Humphrey wanted a more modern house. The great Hall was bleak and draughty and the rest of the rooms went to the other extreme. They were low and dark, and the whole place was thoroughly inconvenient. But they must not stand any longer. Mr. Lovegrove would be waiting.

They went down the hill again and followed the coachway round to the main entrance. The front of the house faced on to a paved court fringed with a green lawn beyond which lay the garden. The heavily studded door stood open, and from it emerged Mr. Lovegrove, a chilly smile upon his melancholy face. They were in excellent time, he said. Her ladyship was gone half an hour since. Would they care to go round the outside first? After that the children might remain in the garden while their father went indoors.

Geoffrey and Barbara glanced at one another. Evidently they were not to be allowed inside the house. But they followed quietly as Father began his survey. Everything was measured already, he said, and his plans were really complete. There were only one or two points he wanted to make sure about, if the new house was to be built on the foundations of the old one.

He called Geoffrey to help him with his measuring tape, and Barbara was free to look about her. But try as she would, she could not make head or tail of the back part of the house. It was terribly confusing. They seemed to be always turning corners or passing under archways or going up or down steps. She was completely lost, and she thought she was miles away when suddenly they came through a narrow courtyard and found themselves at the front once more.

Mr. Lovegrove showed them a seat in the garden, from which they could watch the door and see when their father was ready for them. He did not expect that they would be very long.

Left to themselves, Geoffrey became restless. Why were they to wait outside like lackeys? A bailiff was only a servant himself, when all was said and done. Why should he take upon himself to say that they were not to go inside the house?

Barbara supposed that it was because of illness. Didn't Geoffrey remember what Father had said? Lady Ainsley was afraid that they might bring the smallpox from London.

Geoffrey was peevish. Smallpox indeed! Father was just as likely to bring the smallpox as they were.

Barbara changed the subject. She often did when Geoffrey was getting hot and angry about anything. She had discovered that life was much pleasanter when people did not get hot and angry. So she drew his attention to the front of the house.

It was a beautiful house, she began. Father had spoken of the great hall. Now, looking at it from here, which would be the great hall?

Geoffrey swallowed the bait. He turned and faced the house. It lay across the paved court, warm and mellow in the afternoon sunshine. Dark beams set close together made a framework for a filling of small bricks, sometimes dull rose, sometimes warm brown. The long tiled roof overhung, throwing a deep shadow. Windows nestled apparently without plan among patches of creeper. At each end a wing jutted out, with timber gables and larger windows, a diamond pane here and there catching the light.

Gazing at it, Barbara hardly listened to Geoffrey's lecture.

She was busy wondering how anyone could bear to pull it all down.

Suddenly something caught her eye. She touched Geoffrey's arm.

Look, she told him—up there at the window.

She stared at one of the gable ends. An upstairs casement was open and in the opening stood a strange figure. It seemed to be all in black, the head draped with a long black veil. It stood so still, facing them, that it scarcely seemed alive.

'Is it a ghost?' whispered Barbara under her breath.

As she spoke the figure moved and vanished.

Geoffrey laughed at her. It was just a woman, he said, a woman in widow's weeds; though for a moment it looked like a nun he'd seen in a picture.

A nun? Then it might be a ghost. Perhaps the house was haunted. Barbara still spoke in a whisper.

Ghosts didn't look out of windows in broad daylight, Geoffrey assured her. Look. There she was again, at the other window this time—the little window over the porch.

Barbara shivered. There was something strange about that dead white face among the black draperies. It was close up against the glass, and watching them. She hated it.

Geoffrey told her not to be silly. It was only someone who wanted to see what they were like. Whoever she was, she must have moved pretty quickly to get from that first window to the porch in that short time. Perhaps there was a passage. If so it must be over the great hall.

But Barbara did not care if it was over fifty great halls. It was hateful to sit still and be stared at in that strange way. She got up. She was going to look at the garden. Surely no one would mind if she looked at the garden.

Geoffrey got up too. They went through an arch in the hedge and along a grass walk bordered with tulips and gilly-flowers. At the bottom was a sundial. Barbara stood tiptoe to peep at its face, frowning a little in her effort to read the time. She always found a dial more difficult than a clock. Half after three. Surely Father would be coming soon. She glanced back. But she could still see the face at the window.

Just then Father and Mr. Lovegrove emerged from the door. Instantly the face vanished.

The two men crossed the court. As they turned the corner

of the house towards the village, Father called. Barbara did not need to be told twice. She picked up her skirts for greater speed and ran after them.

Mr. Lovegrove walked slowly. He was deep in conversation. Geoffrey and Barbara followed behind their elders, as they had been taught to do. But Barbara was consumed by curiosity. It was altogether too much for her good manners. She quickened her pace and fell into step beside the bailiff. At the first pause in the talk she ventured a question.

They had seen a lady in black at the window, she said. Please who was it? Was it a ghost?

The Garden

Mr. Lovegrove seemed taken aback. He turned towards her, his long face cold and displeased.

No, he said. It was not a ghost. There were no ghosts at Ladybourne. But little girls should not ask idle questions. He had just been saying to her father that if they remained in Ladybourne they were quite welcome to play in the park. Her ladyship had said so. She was very kind. But he was quite sure that her ladyship would not invite children who pried into matters that did not concern them.

Barbara flushed at the snub. She was perilously near to tears as she caught sight of Father frowning at her. She managed to murmur that she was sorry and bob a quick curtsey. Geoffrey came to her rescue by dropping the measuring tape which had to be picked up and re-rolled.

At the gates Mr. Lovegrove said Good night. He seemed to

have softened a little, for he waited for Barbara to catch up, and repeated that if they stayed in Ladybourne they might go into the park. It extended from the top of the hill right down to the river, and they could go where they liked so long as they were out of sight of the house.

When they parted at the gates, Barbara expected a scolding from Father, but he spared her. Instead he asked whether they were still of the same mind about remaining with Mrs. Jarvis if he went back to London? They might have to be there quite a long time, for there was no telling when Sir Humphrey would return. Mr. Lovegrove had suggested that Parson Hayward, the Rector, might be willing to look after Geoffrey's education. He was a distinguished scholar and had once been tutor to Sir Humphrey. He went twice a week to teach the little girl Elizabeth. If they remained, Geoffrey would have to work hard, and it would be dull for Barbara. What did they feel about it?

Both of them were eager to stay. Father said that he would speak to Mrs. Jarvis, and in the morning he would go and arrange with Parson Hayward. He hoped that they would both mind their manners and do him credit. There was that little business of Barbara's curiosity, for instance. She must promise him that she would keep right away from Ladybourne Hall.

Barbara promised readily enough. She was thankful that her scolding had been no worse. And at this moment she felt that she never wanted to see the Hall again.

Drinking mugs and ninepins

The Joiner's Shop

Chapter Five

EARLY next morning Father and Geoffrey went off to the
Rectory. Barbara remained behind with Mrs. Jarvis. It was
the first time since they arrived at the Wheatsheaf that she had
a chance to look around her. Mrs. Jarvis showed her all over
the inn, and even took her into the taproom, which, she said,
must be out of bounds when the men were drinking. She
would also show her the Travellers' room, but again Barbara
must not go there alone.

The Travellers' room was up another staircase at the far end
of the house, a large and bare room with scrubbed boards, containing only three great beds. It was the room in which they
put travellers who arrived and demanded a night's lodging,
Mrs. Jarvis told her. Every inn had to keep at least two beds
for ordinary travellers. If they didn't they could be called
before the Justices and not allowed to show their inn sign any
more. A tavern, on the other hand, must only serve food and
drink—and not let lodgings at all. In fact, said Mrs. Jarvis,
vigorously plumping up a fat mattress full of hay, they were so
tied up with rules and regulations that they could hardly call
their souls their own.

Barbara wasn't listening very much. Her head was out of
the tiny window in the thatch. She could see Silver grazing

in the field. She called, and the mare looked up and whinnied. Delighted, Barbara decided to go out. Might she?

Mrs. Jarvis said of course she might. If she asked Jarvis on the way he would give her a handful of corn. There were several little baskets hanging up—all home-made—she could take one of those.

Silver loved corn. She followed Barbara round the field, nuzzling her gently to see if she had any more. It was a sunny morning. The light breeze was sweet with the scent of wild flowers. Revelling in it Barbara gathered a bunch of pale mauve Lady's Smock. Mother had liked it when they used to pick it in the meadows at Pinner. Along the ditch in the next field there were Forget-me-nots. Barbara crawled through a hole in the hedge, leaving Silver behind her.

She wandered on happily, regardless of the fact that her skirts were wet and her feet soaking. This was what she had longed for through dull wintry days in London, when the smoky fog made it so dark that she had to sit close to the candle to do her lessons, or stitch a row on her sampler.

Her hands were full of flowers and she was humming softly to herself when a grunt behind her made her jump round. From under a clump of shady trees, its head raised and its tail swinging, came a bull. It walked towards her, slowly but quite deliberately, making a horrible bellowing noise.

She gave one wild glance round her. She could not remember which way she had come. She seemed to be in the very middle of the field. Where was the gap? Where was a gate? She remembered that she must not run; it would only make the bull run too. She tried to walk steadily towards the nearest hedge, glancing back over her shoulder as she went. The bull still followed.

But when she reached the hedge it was as solid as a wall. There seemed to be no way through. Desperately she faced round.

Now she saw to her relief that her bull was only a cow—but a solitary cow, all by itself, and bellowing just as savagely as a very wild bull. Barbara pulled herself together, telling herself that she mustn't be afraid of a cow, and that she must walk quietly round the field until she found a gate. But the cow followed her. It gained on her, getting nearer and nearer, till she could endure it no longer and began to run.

Suddenly a voice hailed her. With thankfulness she saw a gate ahead.

A boy was holding it open, enough for her to get out. She dodged through it just as the cow arrived.

The boy cried 'G'urn' and waved his arms. The cow slowed down, snuffling, and, as the boy closed the gate, ambled away with a doleful moo.

'She wouldn''a' hurt you,' the boy said. 'She's part crazy, 'cos she's lost her calf.'

Barbara was regaining her breath and trying to shake herself back into some sort of tidiness. Now that it was over, she felt rather ashamed.

'Poor thing!' She tried to speak steadily. 'Has the calf been taken away from her?'

The boy shook his head. Glancing at him Barbara thought that he looked terribly poor. He was pinched and white, and his rags barely covered his bony body. He pushed his hair back from his eyes wearily, as though the effort of closing the gate had been too much for him. They hadn't taken the calf away, he said. It had died. Good little calf it was too.

Barbara said how sad. Why did it die? Was it ill?

The boy shook his head again. The old witch had it.

Barbara could hardly believe her ears. *What* had it? she questioned, startled.

The boy repeated in the same weary voice that the old witch had put a spell. She'd let her shadow fall on it, like she did on the young pigs that died, and the hens' eggs that were all addled.

They were walking up a shady lane and Barbara shivered with a sudden chill. Ahead were the chimneys of the Wheatsheaf. She quickened her pace a little.

Was it his cow? she questioned.

The boy nodded. At least it was his mother's, and his mother's pigs and hens too. They'd needed that calf, to send to market.

Barbara wanted to ask more questions, but through a gap in the hedge she could see the road. Father and Geoffrey were walking slowly along it towards the Wheatsheaf. With them was a clergyman with dark clothes and a shovel hat. She suddenly became acutely aware of her wet bedraggled dress. At any cost she must get back to the inn before Father saw her. She said 'Thank you' hastily to the boy and took to her heels.

Carrier's van and trunk

She was in luck; for while she had been out the carrier had arrived with the luggage from London, and Mrs. Jarvis was just carrying her trunk up to her room. The good woman cried out in horror when she saw the state of Barbara's skirts and shoes, but she hushed when Barbara raised her finger to her lips, whispering that Father was just coming and she must change quickly, quickly.

Hastily they undid the baggage and found a clean dress. It was Barbara's favourite, a blue linen embroidered all over with tiny daisies and forget-me-nots. Much washing had faded it and it was getting small for her, but Mother had worked it and Barbara loved it better than any frock she possessed.

While she hooked it up and shook out some of the creases, Mrs. Jarvis hunted for a pair of shoes. But though she found some stockings there were no shoes; they must be in another bundle. Barbara said never mind. If she kept her feet tucked under her skirt Father would not notice.

A peep from the window showed her father and Parson Hayward sitting on a bench outside the inn. Whispering her thanks to Mrs. Jarvis, Barbara crept softly downstairs and out into the sunshine again.

Mr. Hayward was an old man, spare and bent. He wore his own hair which shone like smooth white silk. In repose his face was sad, but when he saw Barbara and smiled at her, a mischievous twinkle lit up his blue eyes.

He looked so friendly that Barbara dropped her curtsey without even waiting for Father to call her. His outstretched hand drew her to the bench beside him. So this was Barbara, he said. He'd heard about Barbara. It was Barbara who had driven in the coach with his old friend Parson Brooksbank of Reading.

Geoffrey arrived with two cans of Jarvis's cider, and while Father was toasting the visitor, Barbara had time to reflect how quickly news travelled.

Parson Hayward turned back to her again. Was Barbara coming to the Rectory for lessons when Geoffrey did? he inquired. Would she like to learn Latin and Greek too, as little girls did in her grandmother's day, or was she going to be a modern young miss and go to one of the new fashionable schools to learn nothing but music and dancing and how to prink in a mirror?

Barbara looked shy. She used to do Latin with Geoffrey when she was tiny, she said. But she'd forgotten it all. And she'd never learned any Greek.

Mr. Hayward patted her hand. Well, well, she should please herself. But she could come with Geoffrey if she liked, and if they did not make a scholar of her, they might make a housewife. Mrs. Hayward was a rare hand at cooking and preserving. She was the village apothecary too, and brewed all her own herbs. He was sure that she cured more aches and pains in Ladybourne than the good man who rode out from Henley.

But, in spite of Barbara's efforts to keep her feet tucked out of sight, Father had spotted her shoes. She was wet, he reproved. Wherever had she been to get herself into that state?

Barbara said she had been into the field to see Silver. Then, to take their attention from her shoes, she went on with the story, about the bull which was really a cow, and how its calf had died because a witch had cast a spell upon it. Was that true?

Parson Hayward looked annoyed. Who had told her that? he demanded. He was so insistent that she had to recount all of it—about the young pigs, and the addled eggs, and the boy who was so poor because his mother could not send the calf to market.

At the end of the recital Mr. Hayward spread his hands despairingly, and looked at Father. What could one do with the people? he asked him. They were just eaten up with superstition. After all, this was the year sixteen hundred and ninety,

43

and one hoped that they were gradually becoming enlightened. But if they were left to themselves they'd burn just as many witches as their grandfathers did.

Father agreed that no educated people believed in witches nowadays. But country folk were slow to change. Probably Ladybourne was no worse than other villages.

Parson Hayward sighed. That was true. All villages were the same. If some poor woman was out of her wits, or was crazed with sorrow, they could say nothing but that she was a witch and lay every bit of trouble—every cock and hen, every pan of sour milk—at her door. He'd preached at them till he was weary of it. If he had his way he'd clap some of them into the stocks. He appealed to Father as if Father knew all about it. What *could* he do?

Father shook his head. He did not know. After all it was only a very few years since everyone believed in witches. Improvement was bound to take time. There had been comparatively few burnings lately. Not many justices would sentence a witch to-day. Soon, probably, none would. Who was this unfortunate boy who had talked to Barbara?

It must have been Dick Colman, the parson said. The Colmans were desperately poor. The father lost his life when a barge was swamped at the weir. It was a difficult bit of river and barges often turned over. But the mother was a shiftless slut. She took to her bed instead of getting out into the fields to earn bread for the family. They were not natives of Ladybourne, and Mrs. Hayward would like to see them sent back where they came from. Every parish had a right to expel strangers if they were likely to become a charge on the rates. But he couldn't harden his heart to do that.

Barbara thought of the boy's white face. He was a very kind boy, she said.

Oh, Dick Colman was a good boy—the best of the family, Parson Hayward admitted. He worked hard and the farmer gave him ninepence a day; that was a lot of money for a boy: more than a grown man got in some parts. He must ask his wife to go and find out about the calf. She often took them some soup or a hog's pudding.

He got up to go, patting Barbara's cheek kindly. He hoped she would be happy in Ladybourne. She must be just about the same age as little Elizabeth Ainsley. They ought to play

44

together. It would do Elizabeth good. She was lonely, poor child. As for Geoffrey, if he came up to the parsonage he would give him some work to prepare.

Father and Geoffrey walked to the corner with him while Barbara, back indoors, helped Mrs. Jarvis to lay the table.

At dinner Father announced that he had decided to ride back to London the next day. Now that everything was arranged for the children, there was nothing to keep him here. He would come down and see them again later on.

Geoffrey inquired about the luggage. It had only arrived by carrier that morning.

Father said that he would leave some of his things here— the plans for the Great House, for instance. By a stroke of fortune, he had ordered a cupboard from Ponting, the village

Stocks and Ducking-stool

joiner, the last time he was down here. It wasn't a fine walnut piece, such as one would buy in town—but just a useful oak press. He'd bought it because it was a good bit of craftsmanship. Now it would just do to keep his papers in. It had a lock, and Geoffrey could have charge of the key.

Geoffrey flushed with pleasure. Where was the cupboard? he asked. Was it here, at the Wheatsheaf?

Father shook his head. It was still in the joiner's shop. They would go down there as soon as they had finished dinner. In any case he wanted to take Geoffrey to see Ponting. He was Mrs. Jarvis's brother and he was doing most of the woodwork for the Great House. He'd got the timber for the rooftree and the joists maturing in his yard, and he was actually at work carving the newel posts for the staircase. From him Geoffrey could learn a lot about the use of timber which would be helpful when his turn came to design a house.

D   45

They went through the village to reach the joiner's shop. The road led them past the gates of the Hall, down a little hill on to the village green. Whitewashed cottages with thatched roofs stood round the green and a party of geese filed in solemn procession towards a pond in the middle. There was a ducking-stool balanced over the pond—a stout oak arm-chair on the end of a see-saw. It looked too comfortable to be a punishment, Barbara said. She wanted to climb into it to see what it felt like, but Geoffrey shouted at her, and Father said gravely that he hoped he'd never live to see her ducked. The justices as a rule ordered it as a penalty for women with rude scolding tongues, who nagged their husbands and quarrelled with their neighbours; and he'd whip her with his own hands before a daughter of his should grow up a scold.

Subdued by the reproof Barbara walked on soberly, stifling a desire to stick her feet through the holes in the village stocks to see what those felt like. The square tower of the church stood among trees. But Father did not go as far as the church. Ponting's workshop lay back from the road, a broad tiled shed with one side open to the air and a straggling timber-yard beside it.

After the blazing sunshine the inside of the shed was cool and dark; and at first Barbara could see nothing. Then, as her eyes grew accustomed to the shadow, she found that the workshop was stacked with woodwork in every stage of construction. A great dining-table took up the whole of one end. A chair stood upon it, its back and arms elaborately carved but the cane still missing from its seat. A pile of wooden posts, twisted like barley sugar, leaned against the wall. Father called Geoffrey to look at them; they were for the staircase, he said. But Barbara's eye was caught by a new cradle, a lovely little thing on carved rockers, and she dropped on her knees to play with it.

There seemed to be no one at home in the workshop, but from the yard outside came the loud rhythm of a saw. Father led the way.

A man stood upon a length of tree trunk. He was working with powerful arms at one end of a great saw which seemed to vanish into the ground. Coming nearer Barbara could see that the wood was laid over a deep pit and that, below, a second man worked the other end of the saw. It must be terribly hard to saw upwards like that, Barbara whispered to Geoffrey, and were they really going right along the length of that tree?

As he caught sight of them, with a warning cry to his partner, the man on the top stopped sawing and mopped his brow. He was a big man, red-faced and grey-haired. His blue eyes and merry smile told her at once that he was Mrs. Jarvis's brother—Ponting the joiner.

He knew that Father had come about his cupboard. It was all ready for him in the workshop. They'd had a bit of trouble with the lock. It had been apt to stick, but Ned had put it right. He was a good hand with locks, that lad.

He led Father back across the yard and Barbara followed. As they reached the shed, he turned and called,

The saw-pit

'Ned! What did you do with that key?'

Looking round, Barbara saw the second man scramble out of the pit. It was only when he stood to shake the dust out of his hair that she noticed that he was not a man, but a boy—a big boy, head and shoulders above Geoffrey, but just a boy for all that, with the gawky arms and big hands and feet of a lad still growing. His face was spattered with freckles and his grin seemed to stretch almost from ear to ear.

He trotted across the yard into the workshop, took a key from a high shelf, gave it to his father, then trotted back again to the saw-pit, where Geoffrey still waited.

Father called her to come and look at his cupboard. She

47

Ned was showing Geoffrey how to cast a fly

had never seen a cupboard like this, he was sure. It was a solid chest of oak with a tiny door in the top half, a tiny door in the bottom, and two small drawers in between. The joiner was proud of it. He didn't know another like it in the south of England, though there were plenty in the north. They were bridal chests up there, in which the bride packed the linen that was her dowry. He'd seen them when he'd been to visit a sister wedded to a Cumberland man. He liked the things, and when he came home he made this one. There was a lot of room in it really. He opened the top door and thrust his great arm in, right up to the elbow, to demonstrate.

Father said that it was just what he wanted. He explained his idea of keeping his plans in it. Had Ponting heard that Sir Humphrey was ill, and the Great House likely to be delayed?

The joiner nodded solemnly. A pretty kiddle of fish, when he'd got most of the timber seasoned, and sawn, and in prime condition.

They drifted into technical talk. Barbara wandered out to look for Geoffrey.

The two boys were chattering hard, and Ned was showing Geoffrey, with a splinter of wood on the length of twine, how to cast a fly for a salmon. Salmon were plentiful this year, and the Thames salmon the sweetest in England, he said. He knew a lot about the river. As well as helping his father with the saw, he also worked for an uncle who was the miller down by the weir. He had a good few tricks for tickling a trout, or setting a trap for a salmon, if Geoffrey could keep his mouth shut. And he helped the watermen too sometimes. They wanted plenty of strong arms to haul the barges up through the flush lock. It was good fun talking to the bargemen. They most of them came from London, and on London river they had really seen life.

Geoffrey nodded. He knew London river; and he started once again the old story of how he shot the rapids under London Bridge.

Barbara's attention wandered. The sound of heavy wheels caught her ear.

An old-fashioned coach, covered with black leather, and blazoned with a faded coat of arms, came lumbering through the village. A stout coachman drove the pair of sturdy well-groomed horses, and the leather window curtain was down. Barbara stood to watch it as it approached. Father and Ponting came out too, Father taking off his hat and Ponting straightening his apron and preparing for a profound bow.

There were three people inside: a thin-faced old lady, very upright, with her white hair dressed high; and opposite her a girl of about Barbara's age, with pale cheeks and dark ringlets. It did not take much of a guess to decide that this was Elizabeth Ainsley and the old lady her grandmother.

The third person in the coach was also a woman, and Barbara's heart suddenly beat faster. She recognized at once the black figure with the flowing black veil. It was the woman who had watched her from the windows.

Quickly she turned and whispered to Ned.

'Who is that in the coach?' she begged. 'The one in black.'

'That one?' said Ned, hardly bothering to lower his voice. 'That's the old witch.'

Barges

Chapter Six

FATHER left very early in the morning. Geoffrey and Barbara walked with him up the long hill to the point where the lane from Ladybourne joined the road to London.

Barbara was sleepy. She had been up late the night before. It was almost bedtime when Mr. Ponting and Ned, with another man to help them, brought the oak cupboard. There followed a long struggle to hoist it up the narrow stairs and into Father's room. When at last she got to bed, Ned and Geoffrey were standing under her bedroom window chattering about London. The wonderful stories that Ned had heard from the watermen had fired his ambition to go there, and Geoffrey obviously enjoyed the opportunity for a little bragging.

This morning Geoffrey proudly carried the key of the cupboard on a riband round his neck. Father had deposited the plans inside and given him charge of them. He had also bidden him take care of his sister, so he wore a slightly superior air which Barbara found vastly annoying.

They waved to Father till Silver carried him out of sight round a bend in the road. Then they made their way back to the Wheatsheaf, enjoying the spring beech woods, and the sense of freedom.

Mrs. Jarvis was looking out for them, and as they came in sight, she beckoned them to hurry.

The chapman was there. He had arrived soon after they

went out, with two packhorses laden with things for sale. He was within doors now, and the wenches were so excited that she could get no work out of them. Of course it wouldn't be such a treat to Geoffrey and Barbara, since they came from London, but to country folk who never saw a shop, the visit of the chapman was a very big event.

London or no London Barbara found the bales of goods enchanting. There was such a variety of wares. In the shops of Cheapside, or even in the New Exchange in the Strand, she had never seen such a mixed collection as this, spread on the great kitchen table. There were shirts and petticoats and kerchiefs, rolls of broadcloth and of baize. There were pins and tapes and gloves, mirrors and brushes and combs, quills and papers, and a long string of news letters and chapbooks that could be read aloud round the fireside and only cost a few pence each.

She peeped between the cottage women who swarmed like flies round a jampot. Mrs. Jarvis made way for her, so that she could stand close to the table. There was a Horn-book which she wanted Barbara to see, a very grand one. It was bound with a silver rim and the sheets of horn were so thin that the letters of the alphabet looked as if they were not covered at all. It had the big letters, the small letters, the numbers up to nine and the Our Father with the capitals all gaily decorated. And look—on the leather back there were pictures of King William and Queen Mary. Wouldn't she like to have it? Surely it was a lovely thing for a little girl!

Barbara shook her head. She had finished with her Hornbook years ago, and no longer used it even to play bat and ball. But something else caught her eye. Lying on the top of the pack was a doll.

It wasn't an ordinary doll, with a silly baby expression. Barbara had outgrown those too. This was something quite different—a very fine lady with a grown-up face, and rouge and patches, with real hair under a fashionable headdress of lace— a 'Fontage' Aunt Anne would have called it: and with a dress all in the latest mode.

Barbara gazed at it fascinated. She had never seen such a doll. If only she had enough money she would love to buy it. She fumbled for her purse.

But when she asked him, the chapman said that the doll was

not for sale. He had brought it specially for the Hall. Her ladyship had ordered it for Miss Elizabeth.

Disappointed Barbara laid it down again. Finally she bought a ball for sixpence; also a little ivory comb and a pair of buckles to fasten her shoes, which she paid for out of her silver crown.

She looked round to see what Geoffrey was doing. As usual he had concentrated on the books. After poring, with a

Doll and hornbook

learned air, over a beautiful leather-bound volume of Tacitus, finally he spent his money on two paper books at sixpence each. They both had pictures on the outside. One was called *The Witch of Marlborough,* and the other *The Prentice who Murdered his Mistress.* Barbara put them down in disgust. Aunt Anne would not let her read about murders, and she did not want to hear any more about witches.

The morning was nearly gone before Mrs. Jarvis succeeded in clearing the chapman and his customers out of her kitchen, so that she could get dinner. Geoffrey and Barbara watched him roll up his bundles and hang them on the packhorses till the poor patient beasts nearly sank under the load. He took with him some of Mrs. Jarvis's best baskets. He'd find a ready market for them, he said, in the country away from the river where willows didn't grow.

When the dinner dishes were cleared away, Mrs. Jarvis offered to show them the way into the Park. There was a little wicket-gate almost opposite the Wheatsheaf. She would put them up some milk and cake for a collation, and then, if they wished, they could stay out till supper-time.

Inside the wicket-gate a trodden path led across the springy turf and over the hill towards the river. The men going to work at the Mill used it, Mrs. Jarvis explained. But they need not go as far as that. She knew a grove of trees which was a perfect place to sit.

The ground sloped gently downhill, a sunny expanse of grass broken by great trees, oak and ash and beech. They left the track and plunged suddenly over the hill-side. It became much steeper and between the trees they could see the glint of water. But after a few moments the ground flattened out again, and they found themselves on a broad natural terrace, sunny and sheltered, with a glimpse of the river curving away through the valley below.

Geoffrey stopped and drew a long breath. What a view! What a wonderful place! Couldn't they stay here? He didn't want to go any further.

Mrs. Jarvis, nodding, put down the basket under a tree. This was the grove she meant. They could do what they liked here and stay as long as they wished. When the sun dropped to the edge of that further hill it would be time to come home.

Barbara waved to her as she topped the slope. Then she looked about. The grassy terrace widened out along the hill-side. There were a few late bluebells. It would be fun to pick a bunch. She glanced at Geoffrey who was still gazing at the view. He seemed quite smitten with the place, and she knew of old that if Geoffrey was smitten with anything it was hopeless to try to get sense out of him. So she set to work on the blue-bells without him.

After she'd picked quite a big bunch, she came back and peeped into the basket. There was a pitcher of milk tied over the top with a napkin, two manchets of bread, split and spread with honey, and two gingerbreads, golden brown and deliciously sticky. Barbara licked her fingers after touching them. She felt hungry already. Would Geoffrey come and eat the collation? But Geoffrey did not reply. He was moodily pacing up and down. Barbara took out the milk and the manchets and the gingerbread and spread them on the napkin. Perhaps if he saw them he would come.

Her plan was successful. Geoffrey threw himself on the ground and devoured a manchet with as much appetite as if he had had no dinner. He said again that it was a wonderful spot. What a site it would make! Think of building a house here. After they had finished he was going down to the river. It looked quite easy to get down. Did Barbara want to come?

Barbara gulped her milk and finished her gingerbread. Of course she would come.

The little path dropped steeply among bramble bushes, but at the bottom they came out on broad well-trodden grass. The river was fringed by reeds and wild-flowers, but beyond them the stream flowed just enough to flatten the blades of rushes. Geoffrey and Barbara wandered along the bank. Further along woods sloped to the water's edge in a little headland. Geoffrey said that they would go on till they could see round that corner.

But before they reached the bend, they were greeted by the sound of whistling. A lanky figure swung into view, shrilly piping the familiar strains of 'Lillibullero'. It was Ned Ponting.

He hailed them cheerfully. He was on his way home from the mill, he said. Were they going to have a look at the weir? They'd come just at the right time. There were two big barges trying to get up it at this moment. He would come back with them.

As they walked along the bank a moorhen fled clucking out of the reeds. She had a brood there, Ned explained, pointing with his finger. Barbara stepped out on a mossy tussock to try and see the nest. But the solid-looking tussock gave way, and only Ned's quick arm saved her from a ducking. She looked down ruefully at her shoes, soaked once more. It seemed as if one always had wet feet in Ladybourne.

Rounding the corner they saw the weir before them. It

consisted of a row of stakes and screens right across the river. Beyond it the water level was higher. A barge lay below the weir waiting to be dragged from the lower river to the upper. One of the screens had been removed, and through the gap the water poured down in a fierce cascade. It was against this torrent that the barge had to struggle. Those men and horses on the bank, Ned explained, were waiting to pull it with ropes, while the watermen on board pushed with poles. The barges were heavy. They were carrying sea-coal from Windsor.

Geoffrey and Barbara exchanged glances. They knew about the coal coming by sea and the barges that brought it up the river. Father had explained it to them at Isleworth. Where was this coal going to? Reading and Oxford and places like that?

Ned nodded. All the riverside towns had coal wharfs where it was loaded on to packhorses. The men who handled the barges were grand fellows. He liked talking to them. Most of them came from London.

Barbara announced that they knew one of the watermen. He had red hair and a patch over one eye——

Flush lock and paddles

Ned's face lit up. That was Sam Pullet. Sam Pullet was a friend of his. Now *he* was a man who had things to tell. His stories were wonderful. And he handled big barges over the weirs better than any of them. Some of the locks were dreadfully dangerous. There'd been a man drowned at this one only a short while ago.

Barbara suddenly remembered the poor boy with the cow. 'Dick Colman's father?' she said quickly.

Ned looked at her. Yes, Dick Colman's father. How did she know?

But Barbara did not answer. Her attention was riveted on the barge which had begun to move towards the gap in the weir. The watermen leaned with all their strength upon their poles; on the bank the team of men and horses tugged with two ropes. Twice it looked as if the barge would be swamped and overturned. But at last it heaved over the weir and steered into calm water on the upper river, while below another one prepared for the struggle.

Barbara relaxed. For the moment it had been so exciting. She wondered if the people in Oxford knew about it when they burned the coal in their fireplaces.

But Ned did not seem particularly excited. To him it was quite an everyday thing. There was a new kind of lock higher up the river, he said. He'd seen them when he went up to Oxford to fetch a load of timber. The barges floated into a sort of wooden pound with big wooden doors. They closed the doors when the barge was inside, and then let the water run in till it rose to the level of the upper river: and the barge just floated out again. It was simple. No pushing and tugging, and no barges swamped. He couldn't think why they didn't have them elsewhere.

Geoffrey listened keenly, but Barbara thought that all this talk about locks was very dull. So she wandered on by herself along the bank. There was a little path that led back into the woods. The sun slanted through the trees on to a patch of blue-bells still in full bloom. Barbara decided that she must have some. Threading her way into the middle of them she crouched on her heels and began to pick.

She had gathered a handful when she heard a twig snap behind her. Quickly she scrambled up. A girl was standing near, a girl of her own size with dark eyes and long black ringlets. She recognized her at once. It was Elizabeth Ainsley.

For a moment the two of them just stared at each other. Then Barbara suddenly realized that Elizabeth was carrying the chapman's doll. As she saw it she smiled.

57

Elizabeth smiled back. Her eyes twinkled merrily and her eyebrows cocked into an elfish line.

'What's your name?' she demanded suddenly. 'I've never seen you before. Where do you live?'

Barbara answered that she lived in London, but just now she was staying at the Wheatsheaf. Her name was Barbara. She'd seen that doll this morning when the chapman came. She would have bought it, she said with a touch of pride, but the chapman said it was sold already. It was a lovely doll.

Elizabeth nodded. Yes, wasn't it lovely? Look, it had gloves on its hands, and real hair. Her grandmother had given it to her. It was her birthday. Had Barbara seen a doll with real hair before?

They stood close together. Suddenly another voice broke in upon them, a sharp high voice which echoed harshly through the trees.

Barbara jumped round. At the entrance to the glade, silhouetted against a shaft of sunlight, stood the woman in black— Ned's 'old witch'.

Barbara felt rooted to the spot. The woman was pouring out at her a shrill torrent of words. She could not understand a syllable. What was she saying? She was talking gibberish. Was it a spell?

As this awful thought crossed her mind, the woman took a step forward. She threw up her arm, as though to drive Barbara away. The arm looked black against the sun. It threw a long shadow—— Barbara suddenly remembered Dick Colman's cow. 'She let her shadow fall on it,' he had said. In a sudden panic, she turned and ran.

Through the trees she fled, back to the river-bank, leaving the bluebells, and Elizabeth, and the woman behind her. There was no sign of the boys by the weir, so she ran straight on, back past the moorhen's nest, back to the little steep path and up to the green terrace.

By the time she reached the top she was completely breathless. The basket was still there. Beside it lay her first bluebells, limp and faded.

She threw herself down panting under a tree, and listened. Except for the song of birds all was quiet. A red squirrel scampered along a branch over her head, and looked down at her with little bright eyes, twitching his bushy tail. But she dared not stay there alone. At any moment the woman might come after her. She would go back to the inn, back to Mrs. Jarvis. If the witch's shadow had already cast a spell on her, Mrs. Jarvis would know what to do.

Without waiting for Geoffrey she bundled the things back into the basket and made for the wicket-gate.

The Chapman

The Kitchen

Chapter Seven

BUT, back at the Wheatsheaf, it was not so easy to confide in Mrs. Jarvis. There were travellers at the inn. The taproom seemed to be full of strange men, and even the kitchen was invaded by a young mother with her two children.

She had ridden pillion behind her husband all the way from Woodstock carrying the baby, while the tiny boy travelled on the front of his father's saddle. Both the children were tired and fractious.

Mrs. Jarvis was busy cooking the supper. A row of bacon rashers stuck on spits were spluttering savagely, while into a long-handled frying-pan, suspended on an iron frame that hung over the fire, she broke egg after egg. Clearly Barbara had no chance of talking.

But the homely atmosphere of the kitchen quietened her. After all, Father had said that no educated people believed in witches. She decided not to say anything about it after all, and contented herself instead by comforting the baby. The poor little thing was hot, bound up by its swaddling bands. She took it from the cradle and played with it until presently its howls ceased and it dropped off to sleep. Barbara was so proud of this achievement that she quite forgot her fright. Even when Geoffrey came in with Ned and asked her where she had vanished to, she only shook her head and did not mention the witch.

All the same she woke in the night with dreams that left

her shaken and terrified. For the first time since she left home, she found herself regretting the familiar background of a London night —the rumble of coach wheels, the padding feet of chairmen carrying sedans and the glimmer of the lights that every house was bound to show till eleven o'clock. Once, at home, she had lain awake with the toothache and heard the watch come round each hour with their 'two o' the clock, a fine night, and all's well'. Now there was

The swaddled baby

nothing to hear except the creepy hooting of an owl or the strange rustlings of something awake out there in the darkness. Not until the cocks, answering one another far and near, announced the first glimmer of day, did she doze off.

After that she slept late. When she got downstairs the men had all gone to work and Geoffrey was already out with Ned.

They were as thick as thieves, Mrs. Jarvis said with a laugh, her arms white to the elbow as she kneaded a great trough of dough. They did nothing but talk about London, London, London, all the time. Ned was mad to go there, and to hear Master Geoffrey you'd think there was no other place in the world. And Miss Barbara was a sleepy head. The travellers had gone hours since. She'd better go to the dairy and fetch her draught of milk. What was she going to do this morning? Would she go and look for the boys, or would she like to help with the bread?

Barbara decided for the baking. She had often helped Aunt Anne on baking days. Aunt Anne had taught her to make manchets. Could she make manchets to-day please?

Mrs. Jarvis laughed. Perhaps. But manchets were a treat. They took butter and eggs and new milk, and were made with pure wheaten flour. Probably Miss Barbara's aunt made all her bread with wheaten flour. Many rich people did. But here

Barbara plunged her arms into the dough

in the country they used mostly barley and rye, with a little wheat to help it. Good filling stuff it was. No one could afford to feed a working man on wheaten bread. There'd be no satisfying him.

Perched on a wooden stool, with her dress caught back out of harm's way, Barbara plunged her arms into the dough.

Mrs. Jarvis gave her a small lump to knead. A lot like this would be much too heavy for her little hands. Had she ever seen so much bread baked before? The bread oven here at the Wheatsheaf was a large one. Probably in London her aunt did not have such a big oven?

Barbara explained that Aunt Anne had one of the new iron cooking-stoves—ranges they called them. But she only baked cakes and pastries in it. All her bread she sent out to the public bakehouse, as most people did in London.

Mrs. Jarvis had pulled the dough into an endless array of lumps and left them to rise, while she attended to the oven. She hooked open an iron door in the side of the great chimney-place showing a wide cavity in the wall. The embers of a whole bundle of faggot wood glowed inside it. Taking a rake Mrs. Jarvis hooked it all out on to the hearthstone. Then she thrust in a wet cloth to swab the oven floor. The water spluttered and sizzled on the hot brick, and the opening was filled with steam. As it cleared she pushed in the dough, loaf after loaf. The door was closed and Mrs. Jarvis glanced up at the old brass clock, standing on a wall bracket, to mark the time. It was nearly ten of the clock, she observed. Wouldn't Miss Barbara like to run down to the Park? Maybe she'd find her brother there.

Barbara hesitated. She did not feel like facing the Park alone, but she had not the courage to say so.

Mrs. Jarvis noticed her hesitation. She also noticed the dark rings under her eyes. Was something the matter? she inquired kindly. Was Barbara feeling homesick, or was anything worrying her?

Barbara swallowed nervously. Then she decided to make a clean breast of it.

It was the witch, she admitted. She was afraid of meeting the old witch.

Mrs. Jarvis wiped her hands clear of flour and set down the cloth with an air of decision. She frowned.

The old witch, she repeated. What old witch? Had someone been telling her silly tales?

Now that she had begun Barbara found it easy to relate the whole story—about Dick Colman and the calf, about the face at the window, about Ned and the day they'd seen the old witch in the coach; and lastly about last night and that dreadful woman in black with her pointing finger and her gibberish.

Mrs. Jarvis listened patiently. Then she shook her head. It was all a mistake, she declared. There were no witches in Ladybourne and Ned was a bad wicked boy to repeat such stories. The woman with the black veil was only Mistress Margot—Madame Margot was more proper, she believed, seeing that she was French.

French! Barbara snatched at the idea. Then was it French that she was talking?

Most likely it was—though in the village they called her Mad Margot—might they be forgiven. Poor soul, she was no witch. Not quite right in the head, may be, but to call her a witch was cruel nonsense. That was the way of people in villages, always chattering and nattering till stories grew like snowballs. She was a foreigner and daft as well; that was quite enough to start them off. A witch indeed! Miss Barbara could hear the whole story if she'd wait half a minute while the pot was filled up to heat. The wenches would want some water to scrub the tables.

With her small hand beside Mrs. Jarvis's big one, Barbara helped to wind the crank that raised a brimming bucket from the well. The fresh cold water was poured into the iron cauldron which hung always on a hook over the fire. Then as she cleared away the remains of the breadmaking Mrs. Jarvis launched upon her story.

Miss Barbara had heard, no doubt, about the poor young Lady Ainsley, little Miss Elizabeth's mother? A lovely young creature she was, and everyone adored her. When she came to the Hall as a bride she brought this French madame with her. Every great lady, the mistress of a fine house, had her gentlewoman who kept her company and helped her with her household tasks. Miss Barbara knew that?

Barbara was interested. Yes, she knew that. A sort of lady-in-waiting—like one of the Queen's ladies.

Mrs. Jarvis couldn't say about the Queen's ladies, but Madame Margot was young Lady Ainsley's gentlewoman. They were cousins, and had been brought up together. When Lady Ainsley caught the sickness she caught it too. She, poor soul, recovered. It would have been almost better for her if she hadn't, for the grief had turned her head. She still lived at the Hall and devoted all her life to her lady's little daughter. She doted on the child, and could scarcely bear her out of her sight. Mrs. Jarvis heard a lot about it because her daughter Jenny was waiting maid up at the Hall. Jenny was fond of Mad Margot. She said she was a gentle mild creature. But it was bad for the child, Mrs. Jarvis thought, to have that poor mad thing in her everlasting black always hanging around.

The well

Barbara nodded. She could understand that. Even though the Frenchwoman was no witch, she still shrank from the thought of those black draperies. But anyway, she would no longer be afraid to go into the Park. She watched Mrs. Jarvis, armed with a flat iron shovel on a long handle, fish a batch of loaves out of the oven, crisp and golden. When they were safely laid to cool, she said that she would go and look for Geoffrey.

She pushed through the wicket-gate with a light heart and ran across the grass. Probably Geoffrey was down by the river with Ned. She would go and see.

But she was wrong. As she neared the flat grassy terrace where they had eaten yesterday, she saw him standing there, all alone, apparently lost in thought.

She plunged straight into the subject uppermost in her mind. With delight she announced that Ned and Dick Colman were quite wrong. The old witch wasn't a witch at all. She went rambling on with the whole story, just as Mrs. Jarvis had told it to her.

Suddenly she stopped. 'Geoffrey,' she said sharply, 'you are not listening.'

Geoffrey turned round. He was sorry, he said. He had been thinking of something else.

Barbara sighed. What was the use of telling him anything when he didn't even bother to listen. It happened so often with Geoffrey. She sat down under the tree and waited. In a

65

moment or two he would start talking, and then she would have to listen whether she wanted to or not.

He began at once. 'I want Father to build the house here, instead of putting it where the old one is.'

Barbara gasped. The new house? Here? Surely he didn't mean that they should build the Great House *here*? It was too big. They couldn't possibly put it right out in the wilds. Look at all the trees, and there was no garden or anything. It would never fit in.

Geoffrey went on talking fast and excitedly. Of course it would fit in. He'd paced it out already—right from one end of the ground to the other. Some of the trees would have to be cut down. But they could be spared. There were plenty more. And just look at the view—'the aspect' he called it, saying the word with a professional air, just as Father did— the aspect was wonderful. As for gardens, they could make new ones, and so much the better. Those little closed-in gardens were as old-fashioned as the house. This site would be perfect for terrace gardens, in the new mode, with the view over the river.

Barbara sat and gaped at him. She'd seen Geoffrey in these moods before, when he pictured himself as another Sir Christopher building cathedrals and palaces, but she'd never seen him quite so much carried away. Where he got his ideas from she did not know. All this talk about gardens in the new mode was beyond her. To her a garden was just a garden. She asked a little timidly what they would do with the old house if they built the new one here?

Geoffrey shrugged his shoulders. The old house? It didn't matter. They could pull it down if they wanted to, or they could leave it where it was. It wouldn't affect the new house, the *Great* House. People didn't build like that nowadays, tucked away in a hollow where no one could see them. They built a house out in the open where it would show up finely. Look at Chelsea Hospital, for instance. Of course Father had said from the start that Ladybourne Hall was too closed in. Wait till he saw this site.

Barbara asked him what he was going to do. Would he write a letter to tell Father, or would he wait until he came back again?

Geoffrey replied that he would wait. He'd like to draw a

plan first, and have it all cut and dried before Father saw it. What a merciful thing that Sir Humphrey was ill, or they might have started work already.

He began to walk up and down, talking all the time about pumping water from the river, and draining it away down the hill, about soils and elevations, about the morning light and the evening sun till Barbara completely lost her bearings.

She let him run on and on until he came to a full stop. Then she ventured to tell him that it was dinner-time. He came quite meekly, suddenly aware that he was hungry.

But on the way back he made her promise most solemnly that she would keep it all a deadly secret. It was terribly important that he should show the site to Father at the right time and in his own way.

Barbara promised readily enough. She loved a secret, and anyway she wanted her dinner.

The Village

Chapter Eight

AFTER the newness had worn off, the days at Ladybourne passed quickly. The village lived its own quiet life very much as other villages did. People rose at dawn and went to work in field or workshop, breaking their fast only with a morning draught of ale or milk and a piece of bread and cheese, enough to last them till dinner at noon. After dinner work again until supper, which was ready as the sun went down, and then one and all dragged themselves to bed for the short summer night.

The summer was a hard season, perhaps the hardest of the year, for no hour of daylight must be wasted, nor would the good housewife permit the lighting of candles if she could help it, since they were usually made with her own hands. The winter would come and, with early darkness, meant a short day's work. That was the time for candles and for sitting about round the fire. Then it was dark at four, and proper for singing songs, or telling stories, or going early to bed so as to lay up a store of sleep against the next summer's toil.

Most of the villagers worked for the Hall, either on the farms or in the woods or at the mill or along the river-bank. A few owned their own small piece of land; four acres were supposed to go with every cottage, so Mr. Hayward told Geoffrey. But though that was the law, in practice a thrifty smallholder acquired more land while a careless one lost his share, and even at the best, four acres were not enough to support a family, so most cottagers went out to earn their ninepence or tenpence a day, which was the wage fixed by the local justices. Everybody worked; even the tiny children toddled to the fields with their mothers.

When Geoffrey went to the Parsonage for lessons in the mornings, Barbara decided to go too. The Rectory was a brand-new house of bright red brick. The Haywards were very kind. The parson set her some exercises, and his wife gave her plenty of occupation. Mrs. Hayward was a bird-like little woman with small bright eyes and a talent for picking up titbits of gossip. Barbara was set to gather herbs for medicines, or beat eggs for an invalid's syllabub; or she could make rush-lights by dipping rushes in hot mutton fat and hanging them up to dry in a long row. Barbara hated this last job. The smell of the grease made her feel sick and the work was never done, for by the time the last rush was hung up, the first was cool and ready to be dipped for another coating.

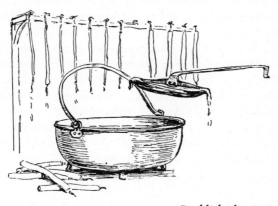

Rushlight dipping

She preferred it when she carried the basket for Mrs. Hayward on a round of visits in the village, though the basket was heavy and most of the cottages smelt horribly. They were like little dark caves to which low doorways were the only outlets, since the tiny sealed windows were filled by thin panes of horn or sheets of oiled linen which admitted only a glimmer of light and no air. Some of these hovels were so dirty that Mrs. Hayward would not let her go in at all.

She was standing one morning outside the cottage of the unfortunate widow Colman, watching all the busy doings in the
village street, when a horseman came riding down the road.
It was Mr. Lovegrove.

Barbara would have dodged out of sight if she could have
managed it. She had no love for the Ladybourne bailiff. But
he had seen her. It could not be helped; she must stay and
drop her curtsey as he passed.

To her astonishment he reined in his horse and called her.
He was searching in a large leather wallet which he carried on
the front of his saddle. After a moment he held out two letters;
one a fat one with a red seal, the other a single sheet folded. He
had been to Henley to fetch the mail for the Hall, he explained.
As the postmaster had a letter for her and one for her brother,
he had brought those as well. Her letter was a single sheet.
It had cost only twopence. But Geoffrey's was a double one.
He had paid fourpence for it.

Barbara fumbled for her purse, but Mr. Lovegrove stopped
her. He had not intended to sue her for the money, he said,
with his wintry smile. Let her put her purse away. Her father
would pay him later.

With a last irritating warning to her not to lose Geoffrey's
letter, he rode away, leaving Barbara to examine the mail.

Geoffrey's was from Father. Barbara knew his neat small
handwriting and his personal seal. She wondered what it said.

Hers was from Aunt Anne. When Mrs. Hayward returned,
she found Barbara with a furrowed brow, struggling to read the
large scrawls and flourishes. Could she help? the parson's wife
inquired; and rather reluctantly Barbara handed over her letter.
Mrs. Hayward read it aloud.

'My Dear Niece. I know you long to hear from me, as I
do from you. I seek occasion to send you a nightgown of indy
silk lined with calico. It will be of use to you to put on over
your night shift when you get out of bed. I have put it into
your Father's hands to wait for a safe conveyance to you. Try
all ways and means to practise on the virginals, that you may
not forget all that you have been taught. I should be very
happy if you could find me a supply of the Rosa Solis for my
cordial against the ague. It is a little hairy plant growing in
marshy places. You may find it near the river. Lay it in a

piece of linen and give it to your Father the next time that he visits Ladybourne that he may bring it to me.

'Your affectionate aunt,

'ANNE KENDAL.'

Mrs. Hayward became quite excited about the Rosa Solis. She could show Barbara exactly where it grew. Sundew was the country name for it. She too used it in her medicines. She would like to compare Aunt Anne's recipe. Did Aunt Anne know that it should be picked on the forenoon of a sunny day as soon as possible after the full moon? Also that it should be distilled in glass and never in pewter?

Barbara was scarcely listening. They were nearing the Rectory and she was longing to give Geoffrey his letter, and to hear what Father said.

Geoffrey did not break the seal until they were alone. He unfolded the two large sheets and read them as they walked back to the Wheatsheaf.

Watching him, Barbara saw his face flush. He read to the end of the letter, then, biting his lip, as was his way when worried, he went back to the beginning and read it all through again.

Barbara could not contain her curiosity. Was there any news? she asked. What did Father say? Was anything the matter?

Geoffrey, his voice unsteady, said that there was plenty the matter. The letter was all about his education. Father had decided that, as he was missing so much of his school time, he should not go back to Westminster at all. As for Oxford, it was out of the question. He could continue his lessons with Mr. Hayward while he was at Ladybourne. He should also go on with his drawing and painting, since they would be useful to him in his future career. In the autumn Father would apprentice him to a Master Builder. If he was to be a successful architect he must first learn his trade.

He handed the letter over to Barbara for her to read for herself.

At the end of it she looked up. Was it really so bad? she asked. Wouldn't being apprenticed to a builder do nearly as well as going to Oxford?

Geoffrey withered her with his scornful look.

Of course it wouldn't, he asserted. Sir Christopher went to

Oxford. He wasn't just apprenticed to a builder; and there had never been an architect to equal him.

Then what was he going to do? Barbara inquired. Couldn't he explain to Father?

Geoffrey shook his head. Explaining wasn't any good. Father just didn't listen. Somehow he'd got to *show* him. There was just one thing that might help. He must work out the Great House on the new site—draw plans of it, and elevations, and finish it so completely that Father would see at once how well he had done it and that it was worth while sending him to Oxford.

Barbara nodded thoughtfully. A scheme was forming in her head. For a few minutes they walked in silence. When they had passed the gates of Ladybourne, and were nearing the inn, she spoke again.

Couldn't he peg out the Great House? she suggested. When Father started a new building, didn't he always mark it out by sticking little wooden pegs into the ground, to see how it would fit? If Geoffrey were to peg out his site, Father would be able to understand it at once. The plans were in the cupboard. It would be easy to get them out.

Geoffrey stopped dead and stared at her. Of course! That was a splendid idea. Why on earth hadn't it occurred to him before? He'd almost forgotten that they'd got the plans. Here was the key—he tugged at a string round his neck. He'd go upstairs at once and get them.

But while they stood talking outside the inn, Mrs. Jarvis put her head round the door and called. Did they not want any dinner to-day? She had put it on the table when she saw them coming. It was all getting cold while they were chattering. Roast duck it was, and if they didn't come soon it would all be finished.

Plans and keys were forgotten in the delights of roast duck with little new green peas, and two kinds of sallets. But while Barbara was still finishing the pastry with fruit conserve which followed, Geoffrey slipped away, and she heard him hastening upstairs to Father's room. By the time that she followed him he had the key in the lock of the cupboard and was struggling to open it.

For some reason the key would not turn. Geoffrey took it out, polished it, and tried again. Then Barbara tried, and finally Geoffrey used all the force that he dared. But it was no use.

They stood back and looked at one another blankly. It was too tantalizing. The plans were inside the cupboard and they could not reach them.

Had he got the right key? Barbara inquired. Could Father have left the wrong one?

Geoffrey shook his head. It had worked perfectly before. Father had made him try it, because he had left some money inside in case they needed any.

Then Barbara thought of Ned. He was supposed to be clever with locks. Perhaps he could open it.

Geoffrey agreed. Ned was the best chance. They'd better go and look for him straight away.

But, it seemed, nothing would go right to-day. They could not find Ned anywhere. His father said that he was down at the mill, helping his uncle, the miller. But when they had trailed in the heat all the way down to the river, they learned that Ned had gone to Henley with a boatload of flour. He wouldn't be back before evening.

Geoffrey returned disgruntled to Barbara on the bank. She was watching a gang of six labourers across the stream. With a tow-rope across their shoulders, they marched single file in slow time. Their tread, dulled by the grass, thudded like the beat of muffled drums, while in unison they hummed under their breath, the inevitable 'Lillibullero'. At the end of the rope a heavy barge glided silently, one man at the tiller, the water gently slapping at its sides.

Barbara and Geoffrey gazed till the procession vanished round a bend. Then Geoffrey called Barbara to come along. It was no use wasting time. They might as well go to the site and cut some pegs ready to start work to-morrow. He'd got his clasp-knife in his pocket.

Even cutting pegs was better than fruitlessly chasing Ned, and Barbara collected sticks for Geoffrey to whittle into shape. She had her skirt full and was wandering about looking for more when a sudden footstep behind her made her turn quickly.

A black shadow flitted away among the trees. Barbara's heart missed a beat as she recognized Mad Margot. She fled back to Geoffrey to warn him that they were being watched. That horrible Frenchwoman was spying on them.

73

Barbara carried the taper

Geoffrey shrugged his shoulders. He did not see that it mattered. They weren't doing any harm. Anyway he was going home now—at least he was going back to Ned's. It was nearly supper-time, so Barbara had better go straight to the inn. She could tell Mrs. Jarvis that he'd gone to see Ned, and he wouldn't be long. Only she mustn't say what he'd gone for. Mrs. Jarvis might wonder what they wanted with Father's cupboard.

Supper was nearly finished before he came back, bringing Ned with him. When the dishes had been cleared away and Mrs. Jarvis and the wenches were washing up, Geoffrey hurried Ned upstairs. The daylight was fading; the cupboard stood in a dark corner, and Ned could hardly see what he was doing. After he had fumbled helplessly for some minutes, Barbara went down to the empty kitchen, lit a rush-dip at the fire, and carried it up.

She held the light for Ned while he prodded at the lock with a bodkin. Just when they were all beginning to feel that it was hopeless, he suddenly touched the spring, the key turned, and the door swung open.

Though the rush taper gave only a flickering light, Barbara could see the end of the roll of plans inside the cupboard, and put out her hand to get them. At the same moment Geoffrey leaned over her. His elbow knocked the light out of her hand. It rolled down the front of her dress with a splutter of burning grease.

'Take care,' cried Ned, and beat out the flame.

For a couple of breathless seconds they all stood in sudden darkness.

She held the light for Ned

But Geoffrey had got his plans. He carried them to the window and examined them in the last glimmer of daylight, while Barbara tried in vain to see the damage to her dress, and Ned fumbled about with the cupboard.

When he had locked the door again, they all three went downstairs. By the light of the kitchen fire Barbara examined her skirt. One glance was enough to show her a large dark stain of tallow grease all down the front. She must change out of it quickly. She fumbled her way upstairs to her room.

Mercifully it was not her beloved embroidered dress, but only a new green sarcenet that Aunt Anne had made for her. What a lucky thing that Aunt Anne could not see it now. She slipped out of the dress, rolled it into a bundle and thrust it into the corner of the little cupboard in the eaves. Perhaps one day she could get Mrs. Jarvis to help her to clean it.

Lych gate

Chapter Nine

THOUGH Barbara was up early the next morning, she found that Geoffrey had beaten her. He was sitting at the table in Father's room working, his coat off, his ruffles rolled back, the plans spread out and held in place by Mr. Hayward's Greek and Latin books.

He looked up as Barbara came in, a rule in one hand, a divider in the other, and a little frown on his brow—just like Father when someone interrupted him. He said that he'd been up for hours. He'd made a drawing of the house as it would look when it was finished, on the new site. Would she like to see?

Barbara's first feeling was one of intense disappointment. The house was hideous—a great high building with two rows of tall windows. There were no pointed gables, no overhanging roofs. Indeed only a little bit of theroof showed over the long straight parapet. Why must he make the house so ugly?

Geoffrey said that she just didn't understand. It was a magnificent house—though perhaps his drawing wasn't quite right in the proportions. Anyway it was Father's design, not his. What *he* had done was to place it on the hill with those trees behind it, and the river winding at the foot. Couldn't she see that?

She nodded vigorously. He'd drawn a lovely *picture*—the river and the trees and all that. It was only the house that she hated. Then, seeing that he still frowned, she changed the subject, and suggested that she should fetch his morning draught and bring it upstairs.

The kitchen was deserted, though the fire had been raked and fed with fresh wood. Mrs. Jarvis was in the cow-shed milking. She told Barbara to fetch two mugs and she would give her some new milk. She could find bread and cheese in the buttery.

The milk was delicious. Barbara had only once before tasted it warm from the cow—more than a year ago in London, when a milkmaid led her cow in from St. Giles Fields and sold the milk, fresh and frothy, from the pail into which she milked it, at the top of Drury Lane.

Geoffrey stopped work to enjoy it. He had almost finished the drawing, he said. This morning they would take the plans down to the site and start to measure it out.

Barbara shook her head. Had he forgotten? It was Sunday. They had to go to church. Mrs. Hayward had told her yesterday that they might sit in the Rectory pew.

Geoffrey's face fell. Yes, he had forgotten. They wouldn't be able to go to the site until this afternoon.

Mrs. Jarvis warned them to be ready early. Mrs. Hayward was very particular that everyone in her pew should be in good time. The coach from the Hall always arrived three minutes before the service began, and the parson did not like people tramping up the aisle after the quality were seated.

So Geoffrey put on his best coat with the silver buttons, and his lace cravat, and took his best beaver. Barbara was a bit uneasy about going to church in her old embroidered dress, when she should have been wearing the green sarcenet, which now reposed in the back of her bedroom cupboard. Mercifully no one here would know which was her best dress, or which wasn't.

The village street had never seemed so busy as it was when they started out with Mrs. Jarvis, wearing a mantua and hood of plum-colour over her Sunday gown of blue kersey. The church bells had just begun to ring, and from every cottage people hurried out—the women in clean starched dresses, and the men looking uncomfortable in coats and neckbands or in stiff newly-washed smocks. A couple of farmers rode up on horseback, their ladies on pillions behind them.

But the sensation of the morning was the arrival of Mrs. Lovegrove, the bailiff's wife, in a sedan chair carried by the garden lad and the stable boy, both perspiring in liveries too big for them.   Mrs. Lovegrove, a wizened little woman with her hair raised on a frame of the latest fashion, was a fine lady from the town, Mrs. Jarvis explained.   She had never forgiven Love-grove for burying her in a remote village and she consoled herself by being delicate, journeying by the stage each year to Bath to drink the waters.   She had returned last time all the way by hackney coach, in order to bring this chair roped to the

Mrs. Lovegrove's chair

coach springs at the back. A pretty penny it must have cost her husband, poor man, Mrs. Jarvis commented tartly. No wonder that he looked as though life had used him ill.

Early as it was Mrs. Hayward was already at her place in the Rectory pew, which was panelled so high that Barbara could only just see out of it.   But the Ainsley pew was higher still, up three little steps.

Just before the bell stopped the procession from the Hall arrived; first old Lady Ainsley in a silk mantua with a scarf of fine lace on her head-dress; then Elizabeth, with a wide straw hat tied over her dark curls, and lastly Madame Margot, still in black from head to foot.   Behind them trooped a line of men-servants and maid-servants who all filed into back pews.

The service was livened by music

The service was livened by music from the gallery. As well as the village choir, there seemed to be a fiddle, a recorder, and an assortment of strange reed pipes which joined in shrilly, more or less at their own sweet will, greatly to the distress of Mrs. Hayward who, invisible to the rest of the congregation, attempted to conduct the choir from within her high pew.

Geoffrey, who had sung in the choir at Westminster under Mr. Purcell, found it hard to keep a straight face, and Barbara had to hide behind her prayer book. Suddenly she became aware of the bright eyes of Elizabeth twinkling at her over the edge of the Hall pew. Just at that moment the fiddle broke a string, and the recorder, startled, emitted a blast like a sick cow. Barbara and Geoffrey both gave up the attempt to behave well and shook with laughter. Elizabeth, evidently pulled from behind, collapsed into her seat with her handkerchief to her mouth.

A withering glance from Mrs. Hayward shocked Barbara into order and she sank down in the pew for the sermon. Mr. Hayward in the pulpit was without his usual smile. He was very dull, thought Barbara. Half-way through the sermon she noticed an hour-glass beside the pulpit. Surely he would end before all that sand ran through. But he went on until the last grain fell. Then the choir broke out again, and Mr. Lovegrove appeared bearing a collecting-box like a warming-pan on the end of a long stick.

The service over they streamed out into the sunshine. Mrs. Jarvis was waiting for them with a rosy-faced girl whom she presented as Jenny, her daughter, who was maid up at the Hall. Indeed all the congregation seemed to be waiting. The black coach stood by the lich-gate. Her ladyship had not come out yet, Mrs. Jarvis whispered. It would be bad manners to crowd the way until they had gone.

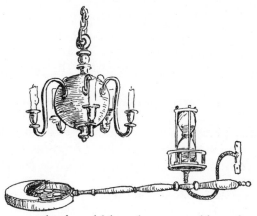

Church candelabra, alms scoop and hour-glass

There was not long to wait. The music inside was still attempting a voluntary when Lady Ainsley appeared, tall and stately, with Elizabeth and Mad Margot behind her. She paused to speak to one or two of the curtseying old women. Elizabeth turned to Barbara and smiled. She seemed as if she was about to come and talk to her. But Mad Margot, who was watching fiercely, seized her by the arm and hurried her to the gate.

The incident was not lost on Mrs. Jarvis. She declared all

the way home what a shame it was that the poor little lamb should be kept without playfellows. Miss Barbara ought to be asked to the Hall to be friends with her. If Mrs. Jarvis could have her way she should go to-morrow.

Geoffrey was walking behind them with Ned. Because of Mrs. Jarvis's chatter Barbara could not hear what they were saying. Their voices seemed to be lowered deliberately. But she could catch a word here and there, and once she clearly heard Ned say, 'I'll take you one day this week.' When Mrs. Jarvis had gone inside to get the dinner, she asked Geoffrey what it was about. Where was Ned going to take him? Geoffrey hesitated. He was so obviously reluctant that Barbara became more curious than ever. At last, after she had given the most solemn promises of secrecy, he told her. There was to be a cock-fight in Henley. He'd never been to one, and he believed it was terribly exciting. Ned often made quite a bit of money at a wager.

Barbara was taken aback. A cock-fight! But they were horrible things. Father hated cock-fighting. He called it a disgusting sight, almost as bad as bull-baiting. At Bartholomew Fair he'd hurried them away from it. Didn't Geoffrey remember?

Geoffrey remembered all right. He knew that Father hated it. But Father was like that. This was a splendid opportunity, because, after all, he was nearly a man now, and he'd have to see things for himself as other men did. Anyway, he was going. And Barbara must remember that she'd given her promise. It was a secret.

Barbara sighed. A promise was a promise. But she didn't like it.

After dinner they went to the Park. Geoffrey had been looking forward to this all day. He armed himself with the roll of plans, his rule and compass and divider, his clasp-knife and a length of tape which Barbara had begged from Mrs. Jarvis.

Barbara, who was feeling sleepy after her Sunday dinner, would have liked to sit quietly under a tree and watch Geoffrey. But he did not give her much peace. There were more pegs to be cut. They had not got nearly enough.

He unrolled Father's plans and began to describe how the house would go. This would be the front. The main entrance

Barbara held the end of the tape

would be here. From here to the end would be sixty feet. That was twenty yards. Their tape was only two yards long. If they tied a peg on to each end of the tape they could keep moving it about.

It really was very exciting. After a little Barbara no longer wanted to go to sleep. The afternoon passed quickly. She held the end of the tape while he stuck pegs into the ground. Before it was time to go home she was beginning to get a picture of the Great House in her mind.

For three days they worked tirelessly, hurrying down to the site as soon as they got back from the Parsonage, and staying there until it was almost dark. Luckily the evenings were growing longer, and supper was later according to the sunset. A forest of little pegs had sprung up and even Barbara could understand the plan as it appeared upon the ground. Geoffrey was beside himself with excitement. It all fitted in perfectly —even better than he had expected. They might have to alter the stable block, but that would not matter very much. Father would be astounded when he saw it.

On the fourth day, though the plan was almost finished, Geoffrey seemed absent-minded as he stuck in the last few pegs. He wanted to be quick, he announced, because he was going to meet Ned by the lock in half an hour. They were going to walk to Henley along the towing-path.

He did not mention the word 'cock-fight' but Barbara knew what he meant. She looked at him blankly. For Geoffrey to go off and leave her like this was something quite new, and she did not think that she liked it. On the spur of the moment she asked if she could come too.

She was rather relieved when he said No. He wouldn't even allow her to walk part of the way along the towing-path. She might fall in, he said. She'd be all right here, wouldn't she? She could have all the collation to herself. Or would she like to go a-visiting with Mrs. Hayward? Only if she did she must be careful not to get asked awkward questions about him.

Barbara shook her head. She didn't want to go to the Parsonage again. She'd just stay and eat her collation and then she'd go home to the Wheatsheaf. Oh yes, she quite understood that she was not to tell Mrs. Jarvis where he had gone.

She waved good-bye to him as he vanished down the little path to the river. Then she sat down by the basket. It was very quiet. Even the birds seemed too busy hunting for food to sing very much; all except a thrush in the distance whose voice rose above the busy twitterings near-by.

As she munched her cake, she studied the plan drawn by the pegs. It was a pity that there were not many more pegs— so that the lines could be continuous, as they were on paper.

An idea suddenly came to her. Why not fill in the spaces between the pegs with little white stones. That would make it just like a drawing. At the bottom of the hill by the river there was a quarry. She had often noticed it. There were lots of little stones there, and plenty of white chalky ones. She emptied the milk-can and the napkin out of the basket, and went down the hill.

She soon found that stones, even small ones, were heavy. She could not manage to carry a full basket. But she made several journeys. From peg to peg she laid rows of white stones. The effect was splendid. As she stood up and looked at it she clapped her hands and gave a little jump of excitement. She no longer missed Geoffrey. In fact she was glad that he had gone. It would be a lovely surprise for him.

The sun was beginning to go down before she finished. On the way home she planned what she could say to Mrs. Jarvis about Geoffrey. She could quite easily announce that he had gone for a walk by the river with Ned. After all that was quite true.

But Mrs. Jarvis was in no mood to ask questions. Outside the inn a great coach was drawn up.

Fiddle, Vamp-horn, Flageolet, Recorder, Bassoon

The arrival of the Duchess

Chapter Ten

BARBARA stood still by the wicket-gate and stared.

This was no ordinary family coach with a pair of horses and a coachman. It was a great gilded chariot with six horses and outriders. Evidently the cortège had only just arrived, for the coach was still occupied. Jarvis, bowing profoundly, scurried backwards and forwards from the inn, while Mrs. Jarvis stood in converse with a fine gentleman in cloak and riding-boots.

Inside the chariot Barbara caught a glimpse of an elderly lady, splendidly attired, with her hair piled over a fashionable commode. A little page held open the door. His back was towards Barbara as she tried to tiptoe unnoticed to the kitchen. But he turned suddenly, and she got a shock. He was a blacka-moor.

Indoors all was bustle and turmoil. Hannah, the kitchen wench, was piling wood on to the fire and poking it to a blaze. Barbara crept up to her and whispered inquiries. What was all the commotion about? Who was it? Were they going to stay the night?

After a backward glance over her shoulder Hannah paused long enough to answer. It was her Grace of Cleveland, no other, with a gallant, and her waiting woman and her page, and the Lord knew what not else.

Barbara puckered her brow. Her Grace of Cleveland; she had heard the name, but she could not remember who she was. Was she a friend of Lady Ainsley's?

Hannah gave something between a chuckle and a snort. A friend of Lady Ainsley's? That was good. Her ladyship would never look at the likes of *her*. That's why she had to come to an inn, instead of going to the Hall as other grand people did. She was driving from Oxford to her house in Chiswick. She had called at the Red Lion in Henley, as was her custom, but the Red Lion had a case of smallpox. So her Grace hurried out of Henley, and came here instead. Where they were going to put them all, and how they were to get food at this late hour, the Good Lord knew, *she* didn't. Would Miss Barbara please move. Tom was killing and plucking chickens as fast as he could, and if she didn't get them on the spits before the flesh got cold, they'd be as tough as old leather.

Barbara slipped upstairs to her little room. Out of all the story, one sentence had struck home. There was smallpox at the Red Lion in Henley. Where had Geoffrey gone? He had not told her where the cock-fighting was to be. How terrible if, after Father had brought them away from London to avoid the sickness, Geoffrey should catch it here. He was not even wearing the hare's foot charm that Aunt Anne prescribed as a safeguard against the smallpox. If only, oh, if only, he would come home.

A hasty peep from the window showed no sign of Geoffrey. But, hidden well to the side, Barbara continued to peep. A procession wended its way from the coach to the door. First came Jarvis, walking backwards. The gentleman in the cloak supported on his arm her Grace the Duchess, her handsome face rouged and her neck hung with pearls. Her gentlewoman and the little black page followed in the rear, carrying wraps and bags and jewel-cases.

Barbara wanted to giggle. From the first glance the painted face with its arched eyebrows and heavy-lidded eyes had reminded her of somebody, and she had just remembered who it was—Elizabeth's doll—the fashionable lady doll that the chapman had brought. Her Grace was the image of that doll, rouge and patches and all.

The next thing to decide was what she was to do. Should she go downstairs, alone, among all that crowd, or should she just stay up here quietly in her room till Geoffrey returned? The worst was that she was getting dreadfully hungry. She decided to slip outside by the back door, and wait for Geoffrey in the road.

The kitchen, as she passed through, was deserted, and silent except for the click of the wheel in the chimney that turned the spits and for the sizzle and splutter of fat as the chickens revolved before the fire. Jarvis, rolling in another hogshead to be tapped, blocked the back door. So she tried the front. But in the porch stood Mrs. Jarvis talking to the gallant and to her Grace's gentlewoman. Barbara attempted to dive quickly behind them, but

Roasting spit

her ribbands caught on the gentleman's sword, and she was brought to a sudden and embarrassing halt.

The gentleman's smile was kind. As he tried to disentangle her, he asked if she were Mrs. Jarvis's little girl. Mrs. Jarvis said 'Oh no, sir,' in a shocked voice, and explained what Barbara was doing at the inn.

When he heard her father's business, the gentleman showed great interest. Building the new Ladybourne Hall, was he? And a friend of Sir Christopher's too? Her Grace would be vastly intrigued. She thought highly of Sir Christopher.

Before she had time to realize what was happening, Barbara found herself in the parlour, making her curtsey. Really, the lady was ridiculously like the doll. She even wore the same lace lappets to her fontage, and the same patches.

Her Grace of Cleveland had a deep vibrant voice and a gracious manner. She put Barbara at her ease, asked questions about her father, called her 'sweet child', and said that she must sup with them. After supper they would have some music. Her Grace adored music. Did Barbara play any instrument? The violin, or the flageolet? The flageolet was charming for a child. Anyhow, of course she had learned to play on the virginals—or the harpsichord, perhaps? That was more in the mode to-day. After supper she must favour them with a performance.

With great relief Barbara said that there were no virginals in the Wheatsheaf. She had not been able to practise since she came.

The Duchess raised her eyebrows. No virginals? In an inn? How, then, did they entertain their guests? But of course she forgot. This was but a country alehouse. She did not often stay in such places. But never mind. Barbara should sing. She had such a soft pretty voice. It was evident that she must know how to sing.

More frightened than ever, Barbara shook her head. She had no singing voice. Her father said that she squeaked like a kitten. But Geoffrey—her brother; he had sung in the choir at Westminster, with Mr. Purcell.

The lady clapped her hands. Oh, enchanting! A boy's voice was quite perfect. Where was Geoffrey? Was he here, at the inn?

Barbara answered that he was out. She almost said that he was in Henley, but she checked herself in time. He had gone to walk by the river, she said. And in any case she did not think that he would sing now. His voice was breaking.

The supper brought in by Mrs. Jarvis and Hannah was like a show of magic to Barbara. She had seen the bare kitchen, with the fire newly stoked to cook the newly executed chickens. She had seen the chickens turning on the spit. And now here they were already roasted golden brown, with a duck done to a turn, a gammon basted with cider, platters of sweetmeats and bowls of cream. The Duchess seated herself in the chair which the gallant placed for her, and said that her hostess had done wonderfully well.

Barbara could not fully enjoy the meal for her eye was always on the window, and her ear cocked for any sound of Geoffrey's return. They had nearly finished before she heard his voice. She waited her chance to beg to withdraw because her brother had come, curtsied hastily and fled, with scanty attention to her Grace's invitation to come back and bring her brother with her.

Geoffrey had gone upstairs, startled by the invasion of the inn, and rather affronted to discover that, since the gallant must share his room, Mrs. Jarvis had arranged for him the truckle bed which he used when Father was there. He wanted to know who these people were, that there was such a fuss about them.

He was slightly mollified when Barbara told him. To her the Duchess of Cleveland was no more than a name. But Geoffrey knew better. With the air of a man of the world he explained that she had been a great beauty at the court of the King—the *old* King, Charles II. Surely Barbara must have heard of her. People mostly spoke of her as my Lady Castle-maine. Every schoolroom chit knew that much.

Barbara did know that much, now that he reminded her of it. She began to fit together what she remembered with Hannah's information that Lady Ainsley would not have her at the Hall. All the same she did not like being called a schoolroom chit, so she turned the tables on Geoffrey by asking where he had been all this time? Had he been to his horrible cock-fight? And where was it? Did he know that there was smallpox at the Red Lion in Henley? She hoped, oh, she *hoped* that the cock-fight was not there.

Geoffrey laughed. She could set her mind at ease. The cock-fight was in a yard behind a tavern—quite a small tavern, nowhere near the Red Lion. It was tremendously exciting, with everyone bawling out their wagers at the tops of their voices. That reminded him. Had she still got the purse of money that Aunt Anne had given her? If so, would she lend him her guinea? He would pay her back without fail as soon as he got some money. He expected that Father would be giving him an allowance soon; he had promised to. But anyway he needed it now.

He was standing in the window catching the last rays of light to re-tie his neckband. Though she could not see his face, she could hear the note of strain in his voice. She promptly asked questions. What did he want it for? Had he been gaming and lost? Was it at the cock-fight?

He rounded on her crossly. Yes, it was, if she must know.

He'd won money at first, but afterwards he lost it. Ned was lucky, so Ned paid up for him. But he would have to pay Ned back. It was a debt of honour.

Secretly Barbara hoped that he would be as particular about paying her back. But she resisted the temptation to say so. Instead she fished out the purse and gave him the guinea.

In the awkward silence that followed, Mrs. Jarvis called up the stairs. Her Grace was asking what had happened to Miss Barbara. She wanted some music. She sent her compliments to Master Geoffrey and trusted that he would honour her with a song.

Barbara had expected Geoffrey to be annoyed. But on the contrary he was pleased. He hurried into his best coat, polished his shoes on the corner of the bed hangings, combed his hair, cursing yet once more that he had no periwig, and told Barbara to lead the way.

Mrs. Jarvis had cleared away the supper and brought lights, in candlesticks of every size and shape. From some corner of the coach the gallant had produced some instruments—a bass viol which he balanced between his riding-boots, a recorder on which the gentlewoman was rather inelegantly blowing out her cheeks, and a lute as a suitable setting for her Grace's long white fingers. A flageolet lay on the table, and the Duchess begged Barbara to try it. She said 'Barbara' with an ingratiating smile. It was her own name, she declared, and there was something delightful in calling so sweet a child by her own name.

Barbara presented her brother, and Geoffrey kissed the jewelled hand with a bow that made her Grace exclaim that he was quite a courtier. He had learned to sing in the Abbey, she had been told. Did he know any of the songs of his master, Mr. Purcell? If so would he favour them?

To Barbara's utter astonishment, Geoffrey did not refuse. His voice was

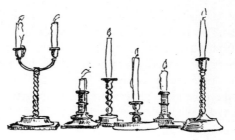

Candlesticks

91

He insisted that Barbara should dance a coranto

breaking, but he knew how to use it in that small room so that none of the wavering notes gave him away. He sang 'Nymphs and Shepherds' very softly, and then, because they were so pleased, he sang it again, for them to follow him on recorder and bass viol. After that Barbara picked out a horn-pipe on the flageolet, and Geoffrey sang again 'I attempt from Love's Sickness to Fly' with her Grace accompanying him on the lute.

The Duchess was enchanted. This was a treat, she said,

which she had never dreamed to enjoy in these wild parts. She made Geoffrey come and sit beside her on a stool—and tell her more about himself, while the gallant insisted that Barbara should dance a coranto with him, riding-boots and all, to a measure on the lady's recorder.

It was an odd dance, but then, said the gentleman smiling down at her, a coranto was often odd, it seemed. Had she ever heard that Claude Duval, the highwayman, had forced a lady from a coach to dance a coranto with him on Hounslow Heath? He must have worn riding-boots too, so they were quite in the fashion. *He* knew all about it, because he had heard the story from Duval's own lips.

Barbara was thrilled. A highwayman? A real highwayman? Did he really mean Claude Duval himself, or was he teasing her? Had he any more stories?

The gallant had plenty of stories about highwaymen, some of them so exciting that she decided he must be making them up. She could have gone on listening to him all night, but after a bit he said that he must see that the coach was safely in shelter.

When he had gone it was very dull. Her Grace had sent for cards, called to the gentlewoman to make a third, and settled down to teach Geoffrey the game of gleek. Barbara decided to slip away.

She went to seek Mrs. Jarvis who was bustling around with a warming-pan for the guests' beds. Though her Grace had seen fit to bring her own sheets, it was just as well to air them, she observed tartly. People felt the cold when they were beginning to get on in years.

Barbara wanted to know how so many visitors could possibly fit in. It was quite simple, Mrs. Jarvis told her. Her Grace would sleep in the best room, with her gentlewoman in attendance. The gentleman would share Geoffrey's room, and the coachman and lackeys would all pack upstairs into the big Travellers' room. In fact Barbara seemed to be the only one who would rest undisturbed. She looked dropping with sleep, poor child. Why didn't she go to bed?

She had not made her duties to her Grace, Barbara complained. Would it matter?

Warming pan

Mrs. Jarvis said that it would not. Her Grace would understand. After all—and a gleam of malice twinkled in Mrs. Jarvis's eye—her Grace was a mother herself.

Barbara had been asleep some time when she woke to find Geoffrey standing beside her bed. He carried a taper, and Barbara, blinking at him sleepily, saw that he was flushed and excited. He held out his hand to her, though she could not at first take in the meaning of what he said.

In the palm of his hand lay her golden guinea. She stared first at it and then at him. Didn't he want it? How about Ned?

Geoffrey said that he had another to give Ned. In fact he had several more. He had won them at cards.

Bass viol

There was someone in the river

Chapter Eleven

THE Duchess and her party were early on the road the next morning. The whole village turned out to see them go. A gilded chariot, let alone a lady of such celebrity as her Grace of Cleveland, was not often seen in Ladybourne.

For Geoffrey and Barbara there were farewells and promises. They must come and visit her Grace in her house at Chiswick. Good-bye—good-bye—— It had been a charming meeting.

With the smacking of riding-crops, a measure on the French horn, and the grinding of iron-shod wheels, the chariot rolled away, leaving the party from the Wheatsheaf waving, or bobbing and bowing, behind it.

There was a sense of flatness when it was all over. Mrs. Jarvis bustled indoors to hurry her household on with the job of clearing up. Barbara looked at Geoffrey, wondering whether she should ask him questions about the gaming last night and the money he had won. But she decided that on the whole it was better not. So she said instead that she was going to write to Aunt Anne. The carrier was calling this forenoon, on his way to London, and he could take the letter. Was Geoffrey going to write to Father?

Geoffrey said that he supposed he had better send his duty. But he really had nothing to say. Everything had much better wait until Father came. Anyway he had no time now. He would be late for Mr. Hayward if he didn't hurry. Was Barbara coming with him this morning?

No, she wouldn't come to-day, Barbara decided. Mrs.

Butter-making

Hayward was going to Reading to visit Mrs. Brooksbank, so there would be nothing for her to do. She would stay and write her letter. After dinner they could go to the Park, couldn't they? She particularly wanted to go to the site to-day.

When she had watched him vanish towards the village she turned back to the Wheatsheaf. The inn seemed so quiet that she regretted that she had not gone to the Parsonage too. Hannah was busy with the churn. Mrs. Jarvis was sorting bedding. So Barbara went upstairs to Father's room and wrote her letter with Father's own writing things. She looked forward impatiently to the afternoon.

She was a little nervous as she crossed the Park with Geoffrey. Would he be pleased with what she had done, or would he say that she had spoiled his beautiful plan? Well, anyway it would be easy enough to take her white stones away again if he did not like them.

But Geoffrey was delighted. The surprise was just as complete as she wanted it to be. He was talking about her Grace of Cleveland until they got quite close to the site. Then as they came over the slope of the hill he stopped dead and stared.

The pattern on the ground stood out with startling clearness. The ground plan of the Great House looked immense, stretching almost from end to end of the green terrace.

At first he couldn't believe that Barbara had really done it all. He was startled out of his usual superior elder-brother attitude. It was wonderful, he exclaimed, as Barbara breathlessly described her afternoon's work. Why, anyone could understand the plan at a glance now.

He hurried down the slope and stood on the neat square which was to be the porch.

Look, he declared, you could actually go in at the front door, cross the hall, stand at the bottom of the grand staircase. Then you could turn to the right and go into the saloon, or turn left and into the library—or out on to the terrace to admire the view.

He picked his way from room to room as he talked, while Barbara stood, thrilled with delight that it was such a tremendous success.

Where did she get her stones? he wanted to know. It would be worth while getting some more and making a double row for the outer walls. He thought, too, that the doors and windows might be a bit clearer. To-morrow he'd bring Father's plans again.

Barbara led him down the path to the river and showed him the gravel pit. It was a pity that they had not brought a basket. Would it be worth while going back to fetch one?

Geoffrey thought it would. Then he had a better idea. There were some baskets at the mill—big ones with two handles. If they went along there Ned would let them have one, and they could drag it up the hill between them. Anyway he wanted to see Ned and give him his guinea.

Barbara warned him that a big basket wasn't much good. The stones were too heavy. But Geoffrey wouldn't be put off. He strode along the bank so fast that Barbara had all that she could do to keep up.

They rounded the bend in time to hear a cry and a loud splash. It came from the direction of the bed of reeds where Barbara had once nearly fallen in. They started to run. That cry could only mean one thing. There was someone in the river.

Suddenly Geoffrey took a flying leap. Barbara screamed. The reeds prevented her from seeing what was happening, though the upheaval of the water swept out in widening circles to the middle of the stream.

But almost immediately Geoffrey came stumbling back, soaked from head to foot, and supporting a wet and weeping girl. It was Elizabeth Ainsley.

Water streamed from her clothes and her dark curls hung in rats' tails. Barbara tried vainly to wipe the mud and slime from her face with her own handkerchief.

They must get her home quickly, Geoffrey said. He would run to the mill and get help—someone who could take her back to the Hall.

But Elizabeth had recovered enough to understand. Between her gulps and sobs, she shook her head violently, crying 'No—no'.

Geoffrey and Barbara looked at one another. What was to be done?

Barbara did her best to be soothing. What was it? she inquired. Had she been trying to see the moorhen's nest? That bank was terribly dangerous. She'd nearly fallen in herself a little while ago.

Elizabeth mopped her face again, and explained that she had been running away. It was Margot who drove her to it. Margot said she wasn't to go near the river. Margot was always saying she mustn't do this, or mustn't do that. So she ran away. And she wouldn't go back now, all wet like this—no, she *wouldn't*—she stamped her foot on the bank. Margot would see her and she'd scold and scold, and probably she'd tell Grandmother. She must get dry before she saw Margot.

Her teeth were beginning to chatter, and Geoffrey, who was shivering himself, said that she mustn't stand still like this—she'd catch her death. If she wouldn't go home, they'd better take her to the Wheatsheaf.

Elizabeth nodded, trying to push her wet hair out of her eyes; and Geoffrey led the way, along the river-bank and up the steep path, climbing so quickly that they could not keep up with him. At the top they saw him running ahead towards the inn, and just as Barbara guided Elizabeth through the wicket-gate, Mrs. Jarvis came hurrying out to meet them.

She wasted no time asking questions but bundled Elizabeth across the road and into the kitchen. Hannah had already got the bath-tub out by the kitchen fire, and was pouring water into it, while over the flames the big cauldron steamed. Mrs. Jarvis briskly began to take Elizabeth's wet clothes off her. She told Barbara to run upstairs and bring down some of her own things. They would fit Miss Elizabeth near enough.

Barbara obeyed. She hunted out a clean shift, a set of underclothes, a petticoat, and her warm blue dress—the one that she had worn on the journey down from London.

When she got downstairs again Elizabeth was already out of the tub and Mrs. Jarvis was rubbing her wet head vigorously with a dry towel. Afterwards when she was sitting wrapped in a blanket by the fire, and Mrs. Jarvis was preparing a hot cordial, she looked at Barbara and laughed.

It was fun, she said, her dark eyes dancing with mischief. Margot had said that she wasn't to go near Barbara. Margot

Mrs. Jarvis was rubbing Elizabeth's wet head

had made a terrible to-do every time she had spoken to Barbara. And now here she was, wearing all Barbara's clothes.

The spell was broken and they both laughed and chattered and compared notes, till Mrs. Jarvis brought the hot cordial. It was so nasty that, while Mrs. Jarvis went to find Tom, the yard boy, and send him galloping up to the Hall, Elizabeth tried to make Barbara throw it out of the window. When Barbara wouldn't she got up herself, tottering in her blanket, and poured it into the bath-tub. It made the water look pink, and the steam smell of cloves and peppermint. Elizabeth pretended to be fainting with heat so that Barbara could open the window and let some of the smell go out.

When Mrs. Jarvis came back, Elizabeth said she was beautifully warm now, and please she was so hungry.

So Mrs. Jarvis brought a collation of milk and manchets and gingerbread and some marchpane which Elizabeth declared was the most delicious she had ever tasted. She would love to know how it was made. So, laughing, Mrs. Jarvis produced ground almonds and bread-crumbs, and they all, including Geoffrey, got gloriously sticky moulding it into shapes with honey. It was set to bake in a cooling bread oven.

They were all happy in the kitchen—especially when Hannah, clearing the tub away, spilled some of the water, and Mrs. Jarvis sniffed the air, saying she must have trodden on a clove. Barbara told Elizabeth about the visit of her Grace of Cleveland, and Geoffrey made them all laugh with his imitation of the gallant dancing a coranto in riding-boots.

He was in the middle of this display, when the old black coach drove up to the door to fetch Miss Elizabeth.

Elizabeth did not want to go, but Jenny, Mrs. Jarvis's daughter, had come with the coach, bearing a load of shawls and rugs to wrap her in.

So, much against her will, she was rolled up and taken out, and the last that Barbara saw was her hand waving between the leather curtains of the coach, while she cried out that whatever Margot said, she would see Barbara again soon.

As they went back to the kitchen, Barbara remarked it was odd that they should have been waving good-bye to two coaches in one day.

Writing materials

The Great Hall

Chapter Twelve

THE next morning was wet, which was a disappointment. Geoffrey had two days' holiday from the Rectory, and he had planned to spend the time at the site, finishing the work that had been interrupted by Elizabeth's adventure. But the rain poured down, and reluctantly he settled himself to his Greek and Latin books.

Mrs. Jarvis declared that the rain would not last. So Barbara kept a sharp look-out from the window to see if there were still splashes in the puddles. About ten she announced that it had stopped. Geoffrey told her to go on watching. They'd give it another half-hour to clear up and then they would go out. It would be wet in the Park, but they could go round by Ponting's or down to the mill. He still hadn't seen Ned to pay his debt.

Long before the half-hour was up, Barbara called him to come to the window—quick, quick. Mr. Lovegrove had just arrived. And he had an *umbrella*.

Geoffrey came at once and peeped through the diamond panes. Mr. Lovegrove certainly did look funny balancing a

large umbrella of striped ticking with a heavy fringe from which the water dripped. He'd get more wet from the umbrella than he would from the rain, Barbara remarked. What a silly thing to use. Surely they were meant to keep off the sun?

Geoffrey explained that they were originally intended for sun, but quite a lot of people in town used one for rain. Only they usually had a lackey to carry it.

Mr. Lovegrove crossed the yard to the door of the inn. They heard his voice calling to Mrs. Jarvis.

What had he come for? Barbara wondered. Perhaps he had brought some more letters. After a few minutes Mrs. Jarvis came to the bottom of the stairs and called them. Would they be pleased to come down? Mr. Lovegrove wished to speak with them.

Barbara was a little worried as she followed Geoffrey downstairs. Since that first day she had never connected Mr. Lovegrove with the thought of anything pleasant.

Mr. Love-
grove's
umbrella

But Mr. Lovegrove's melancholy face held the ghost of a smile. He had come on an errand for her ladyship, he began. It was a very pleasant errand. Her ladyship had heard how Master Geoffrey saved the life of Miss Elizabeth yesterday by pulling her from the river—a most praiseworthy action. Her ladyship would be glad if Master Geoffrey and his sister would come up to the Hall so that she might offer thanks herself. He had been sent to conduct them. If they were ready he could take them now. They were invited to remain to dinner.

They hurried to tidy themselves. Barbara had no dress to change into, as the green sarcenet was hidden in the cupboard and Elizabeth had her warm blue one. But she hastily changed her white cambric smock, because the frills at the neck and sleeves, which showed beyond her bodice, were far from being the snowy white that Aunt Anne insisted was the mark of a gentlewoman.

Mr. Lovegrove led them through the main gates and along the drive. They had not been that way since the first day with

Father. He walked slowly talking of Ladybourne, and of the problem caused by Sir Humphrey's illness. There was a new trouble to-day. Thanks to the war with France, an order had come that the Militia guard must be ready in case of invasion. Sir Humphrey was responsible for the local Militia, and in his absence his duty fell upon his bailiff. He could assure them that it was no joke to make all the village men attend to their drills and their training.

The clouds had broken up by now. The sun was out, and in the clear light after the rain, the old house looked just as beautiful as on the day they first saw it.

Mr. Lovegrove left them standing in the porch while he went to see if her ladyship was ready to receive them. He was back in a few seconds, telling them to follow him.

The door opened into a dim passage, lighted only by a panelled screen. Through the screen they looked into the hall, a great lofty room reaching to the roof, with a dais at the far end and a large fireplace at the side.

Alone in the hall sat Lady Ainsley, busy at a spinning-wheel. Her high-backed chair was placed on the single Turkey carpet near the hearth. With the exception of a large table and some straight-backed chairs on the dais and a livery cupboard against the wall, the room was empty. There was a frightening expanse of floor to be crossed to reach Lady Ainsley.

Barbara looked round for Mr. Lovegrove, but Mr. Lovegrove had, apparently, left them to present themselves. Geoffrey developed an unwonted shyness. So Barbara took a deep breath, and, seizing his hand, led the way through the screens into the hall.

Lady Ainsley looked up from her work to smile at them and Barbara dropped Geoffrey's hand again to complete her best curtsey. When she smiled, Lady Ainsley, so tall and so dignified with her white hair brushed from her forehead, ceased to be frightening.

Speaking slowly, in a voice that was deep and quiet, she said that her granddaughter had described how they had rescued her from the river—in fact, if Geoffrey had not been there Elizabeth might have been drowned. She still did not know quite what had happened. She believed that Elizabeth had been naughty and had run away from her cousin. But nothing could alter the fact that she owed her life to Geoffrey.

Stammering and blushing, Geoffrey declared that he had done nothing worth mentioning. It was just good fortune that he happened to be there. The bank was dangerous. It was easy to slip in. His sister had nearly done so a little while ago.

Lady Ainsley put them at their ease. She asked about the Wheatsheaf. Were they happy there? She was sure that Mrs. Jarvis was good to them. And had their father been down to see them lately? It was unfortunate that the building had been put off—though for herself she supposed she should be thankful. It had given her a few more weeks in her old home. She had no doubt that the new house would be very fine, but to her it could never make up for the old one.

Barbara agreed, saying 'Oh *No*' so eagerly that Lady Ainsley looked at her in surprise. Did she like the old house then? She would have expected their father's children to prefer modern places.

Oh, but this house was *lovely*, Barbara cried, and Geoffrey looking round him, said that the Hall was beautiful.

Lady Ainsley set aside her spinning-wheel. If they loved the old house so much they must go over it.

She clapped her hands and when a bobbing serving-maid appeared, she told her to find Miss Elizabeth. Then she turned to show them the Hall.

It was the oldest part of the house, she explained. When it was built it was the general living-place of everyone in the household. The lord of the manor and his lady may have had their private room—the 'Solar' they would have called it. It was still there, beyond the dais; it was known as the parlour now. But everyone else just slept round the fire. There was no fireplace at first. The fire was built in the middle of the room. If they looked up they could see the patch of darkened wood where the smoke used to go out.

They walked slowly round, looking at a fine tapestry of some people hunting a deer, at the coats of arms in the big window that lighted the dais, and at the line of portraits on the further wall, beginning with a funny old-fashioned one of a lady in a stiff ruff, and ending with a modern picture of a fair gentleman in a periwig. That was Elizabeth's father, my lady told them. Her mother's portrait should have hung beside it, but alas! it was never finished.

She led them across the dais and through a door at the end.

Here was the parlour, she said—the room that used to be called the Solar in the old days. This was probably the only private room, when the house was built—though it had a little sleeping-room over it.

The room was small and dark. Its walls were panelled with oak—Geoffrey called it the linenfold pattern. He was studying it when Elizabeth came in, rather breathless. She dropped a hasty curtsey to her grandmother and instantly seized Barbara's hand. She was so glad they had come, she said. There was so much that she wanted to show them. Please might they go?

Elizabeth's toys

Lady Ainsley told them to be off. But the dinner bell would be sounding soon. They had better not go far.

Elizabeth led them through the hall, up a staircase beyond the screens, and into a pleasant room which she said was her nursery. There was a fireplace, a large table and some wooden stools, a high-backed oak settle littered with toys, and beside it Elizabeth's old nursery chair. Of course she had quite out-grown that chair, Elizabeth explained apologetically, as she swept a space on the settle for them to sit down. And some of the toys were very babyish too. Her grandmother said she should give them away to the poor, but somehow she did not like parting with them.

In the meanwhile Geoffrey had gone to the two windows which looked on to a courtyard at the back. He was puzzling out the geography of the house, with the little furrow between his brows which he always had when he was 'set' on anything. After a few minutes he called to Elizabeth to help him: they had been long enough over a stupid doll.

He wanted to know what was that wing built out on the left? The one on the right was the kitchens, he could see that; and the hall door was beside them. But what was the left-hand one? It had another long roof-tree, though it was probably built later, judging by the squared arch.

Elizabeth said that it was the library. It used to be an old chapel, but as they all went to church in the village, Father had made the downstairs part into his library. There were lots and lots of books. Would he like to come and see?

She took them downstairs again, and out by a back door. But they were only half-way across the courtyard when a bell rang out from a little belfry up on the gable end.

Dinner in ten minutes, said Elizabeth. They had better go at once, for Grandmother liked them to be there when the household came in.

To Barbara's astonishment the hall had been completely transformed. The table on the dais was covered by a white cloth, and spread with silver and pewter and glass, polished till it reflected the colour of the coats of arms in the big window. Down in the body of the hall, formerly so bare, a long trestle table had been set up, with wooden benches beside it, and mugs and platters, and knives and spoons on it. Mrs. Jarvis's daughter Jenny, her rosy face wreathed in smiles, stopped in her task of filling the mugs with beer, and bobbed to them as they passed.

Lady Ainsley, who awaited them in the parlour, led the way to the dais. Barbara sat at one side of her hostess and Geoffrey at the other. Beyond him stood an empty chair. Barbara cast sidelong glances towards it. Who was to sit there? Would it be Mad Margot?

From the screen at the other end of the hall the servants filed in, a long line of maids in holland dresses and a string of men with clean smocks hastily pulled on over their working clothes.

After Lady Ainsley had said grace the dishes were presented in livery cupboards—closed on three sides to keep the food hot. Old Giles, the white-haired butler carved for the high table, the servants at the trestles waited patiently until the family was served.

The platters were still being handed round when the door at the back of the dais opened, and Madame Margot came in. Her face looked very white under the black veil, and her eyes roamed keenly round until they rested on Barbara and Geoffrey. For a moment she stopped dead. Then she recovered herself, dropped a curtsy to Lady Ainsley and babbled an apology in French. Barbara was thankful that her seat was at the other end, and that she was hidden except when the Frenchwoman deliberately leaned forward to peer along the table.

Geoffrey had completely overcome his shyness. He talked to my lady quite happily. Barbara could hear him telling her about Westminster, and about Oxford and how he longed to go there. For herself, she did not want to talk. It was the first time she'd dined in a hall in the old-fashioned way. There was so much to look at. She was quite sorry when the last grace was said and the family withdrew to the parlour.

As soon as Lady Ainsley was settled, she sent Elizabeth to fetch her embroidery frame. She was working a new hanging for Elizabeth's bed—curtains and valence, covered with a heavy design of fruit and flowers. Elizabeth herself was doing the cover—at least she had *started* the cover, her grandmother said with a smile; but doubtless it would have to be finished by other hands if Elizabeth was to use it this side of the grave. Was Barbara a good needlewoman? She would not have much difficulty in putting Elizabeth to shame.

Barbara thought of a rather grubby and crumpled sampler which she had carefully left in London, and was not so sure. But she was spared the necessity of replying by the arrival of Jenny Jarvis, bearing a tray!

Tea! my lady remarked with a smile. A dish of tea after dinner was her pet extravagance. Did Barbara like tea? No? It was an acquired taste, of course. Elizabeth did not care for it either.

Elizabeth wrinkled her nose in disgust. Horrible stuff, she declared. She would as soon drink dirty water.

There was no need, her grandmother reassured her, the tea-pot in her hand. Tea at twenty-five shillings a pound was not to be forced on little girls who did not like it. She and Margot would enjoy theirs in peace.

But Madame Margot was not paying attention. Ever since they left the dining-hall her eyes had wandered first to Barbara,

then to Elizabeth, then back to Barbara again. They made
Barbara feel shivery. She wished that she would not stare like
that. At last, able to bear it no longer, she whispered to Elizabeth. Why did Madame Margot look at her like that? she asked.

Elizabeth glanced round. But instead of answering Barbara,
she said something quickly in French.

The effect was immediate. The Frenchwoman suddenly
and without warning burst into tears. She turned to Lady
Ainsley, chattering and waving her hands. Then she made for
the door.

But before she reached it she swung round again and made a
sudden dart at Geoffrey.

'You have saved her; you have saved her,' she cried in broken

Still-room

English. To his obvious horror, she seized him by the shoulders,
kissed him firmly on both cheeks, and rushed from the room.

For a moment there was an embarrassed silence, broken only
by Elizabeth's giggle. Then Lady Ainsley began calmly to
explain.

They must take no notice of Madame Margot. She often
had these attacks. She was devoted to Elizabeth—more devoted
than Elizabeth deserved, the heartless child, and she was sus-
picious if Elizabeth made new friends. But she would soon
grow used to Barbara. As for Geoffrey—she knew that he
had saved Elizabeth's life, and therefore she was his servant for
ever.

They all laughed at that, and Lady Ainsley asked them
quickly what they were going to do this afternoon? Had

Elizabeth showed them all the house? Then perhaps they would like to go outside. Would they care for a game in the bowling alley? It was a pity to remain within doors on such a lovely day.

Geoffrey would have preferred the library, but he did not like to say so. So out they went. First they explored the confusing clusters of barns and buildings round the back of the house—buttery, dairy, bakehouse, laundry, stables, brewhouse. The most fascinating of all was Lady Ainsley's still-room where she made preserves and cordials and perfumes, as well as the extracts of herbs and precious medicines that kept her household healthy. The still itself was built round a little charcoal stove and its glass retort earned Geoffrey's warm praise. It was, he declared, good enough for a chemist's laboratory.

By the time that they had offered their thanks to my lady, and waved good-bye to Elizabeth, Barbara's mind was in such a whirl that she could not remember half that she had seen.

Geoffrey was serious and thoughtful as they walked back through the Park. It was a shame to pull down that old house, he observed—even for the sake of building the new one. Now, if only Father would agree to his site, it wouldn't have to be pulled down at all. They could keep both houses.

Why didn't he tell Lady Ainsley? Barbara urged. Or why not write a letter to Father? Surely it couldn't hurt to write a letter?

But Geoffrey shook his head. He knew best, he maintained. He must choose his time carefully. When Father was in a good mood, he must take him to the site. There was no other way. The very first thing was to finish laying it out with the white stones. When it was quite perfect, they must cover it up with dead leaves, so that no one passing would notice it, and just wait patiently till Father came back again.

At the inn Mrs. Jarvis was on the look-out for them. She seemed worried.

She wanted to know if they had seen Ned? He had been missing all day. In fact he'd not been home since last night and his mother was in a terrible state. She thought perhaps that Master Geoffrey might know something?

Geoffrey shook his head. No. He'd not seen Ned since they went to Henley together three days ago.

Mrs. Jarvis sighed. She was disappointed. She did hope

that Master Geoffrey could have helped. They would have been frightened about the river except that he had put on his best clothes. That looked as if he'd gone deliberately. And, another strange thing, Dick Colman was missing too.

Barbara stared at her. Dick Colman? That poor boy who'd lost the calf? But surely he couldn't leave his mother.

Well, he *had* left her, Mrs. Jarvis asserted. That's what made people wonder if they hadn't been kidnapped. All except Ned's best clothes. It was a regular puzzle.

As soon as they were alone, Barbara looked at Geoffrey. She had a queer feeling that Geoffrey knew more than he said.

But Geoffrey shook his head. He didn't know. They had said nothing to him. But Dick Colman had been with them at the cock-fight the other night, and had won money too—quite a lot of money. He wouldn't be a bit surprised if Dick and Ned had decided, on the strength of their winnings, to go off to London.

Barbara gasped. To London? But why? Did they know anyone there? Had they got anywhere to go?

Again Geoffrey shook his head. He didn't know. But Ned was crazy to go to London. He was always saying if he could only get to London he would make his fortune.

Barbara frowned. If Geoffrey was so certain, oughtn't he to tell Mrs. Jarvis?

Still Geoffrey said No. It wouldn't do any good. He didn't *know* anything. They hadn't actually told him. All the same, if they were still missing by the morning, he might tell her then.

Chapter Thirteen

BUT in the morning Mrs. Jarvis greeted them with the news that a note from Ned had been found in Ponting's workshop. It had blown down and been overlooked the night before.

Ned and Dick Colman really had gone to London. There was no cause for anyone to worry, Ned wrote. They had money in their pockets, and by the time that it was spent they would have earned more. They both wanted to get rich and Dick would send money home to help his mother.

Mrs. Jarvis was very upset. London was a wicked city, she declared, and no place for a couple of friendless lads. Of course Ned's father had gone after them as soon as he'd read the letter, but what was the use? He'd never know which way to look. They'd taken a horse from Farmer Whitgrave, Colman's master, so they'd likely be there by now.

Taken a horse, Barbara repeated. They couldn't both ride one horse. They were too big and heavy.

They could 'ride and tie,' Mrs. Jarvis said. That was the way many country folk travelled. First one took the horse and rode ahead. Then he dismounted, tied up the horse, and walked on. When the second one reached the horse he mounted and caught up the first. They covered far more ground like that than if they both had to walk all the time.

Geoffrey thought it was a fine idea. Barbara could see that he was very thankful that he'd not been obliged to break the news about London.

As soon as Mrs. Jarvis had gone back to her work, Geoffrey started bustling round. He wanted to get to the site early, he told Barbara. There was a lot to do. He was going to bring Father's plans to-day, so that when they had finished placing the white stones, they could check it again and make sure that it was accurate before they covered it up with leaves.

When they reached the site they spread out the plans and held them flat on the ground with four large stones.

Really, it was very good, Geoffrey remarked proudly, standing back to compare their handiwork with Father's design. There wasn't very much more needed to make the outer walls distinct, and then they could start collecting leaves. He'd feel happier when it was hidden from prying eyes.

Among the trees there were several dips in the ground full of last year's beech leaves, dry and crisp. Geoffrey scooped them up and Barbara carried them in her skirt.

They had worked hard for some time, and the white stones were nearly all covered, when Barbara looked up and saw that the sun was exactly overhead. Noon! She gave a sigh of relief. Her arms were aching. She called to Geoffrey that it was dinner-time.

But Geoffrey hung back. He wanted to finish. It would only take a few minutes.

Barbara was impatient. They'd done enough for now. She was simply starving, and Mrs. Jarvis hated them to be late.

Geoffrey came grumbling. They had reached the wicket-gate when he stopped dead. Father's plans! They had left them on the ground.

They'd be all right, Barbara insisted airily. Dinner didn't last long, and nobody would be likely to go that way. If he went back now they'd be terribly late.

Geoffrey ate his dinner in a hurry, and Barbara, who would have liked a second helping, caught his eye and thought it wiser to refuse. He even started back across the Park without her, and she had to run to catch him up.

She was still panting when he suddenly cried 'Look!' and pointed straight ahead.

Among the trees in the distance a dark figure moved. There was no mistaking those black draperies. It was Mad Margot.

She was walking away towards the Hall. Of course she might not have been to the site, but anyhow she must have passed quite near it.

Geoffrey quickened his steps. He did not like that woman, he said. She was always poking and prying somewhere.

At any rate she had not done any harm, Barbara remarked,

as they came over the top of the hill. Everything looked just as they had left it.

But Geoffrey cried out in dismay.

Father's plans had gone.

They searched high and low—hoping against hope that they had blown away, and were caught up in a bush. But there had been no wind. And what was more, the four large stones which had kept the roll flat were lying all together in a neat heap.

Only one answer was possible. Mad Margot had taken the plans.

Geoffrey was distracted. He paced up and down looking at the ground, as if, by magic, they would appear at his feet. Barbara thought he should go straight to the Hall and get them back, but he said No. They must think first. If he went to the Hall and saw Lady Ainsley or Mr. Lovegrove, they would want to know what he was doing with the plans. Then it would all come out, Father would be angry and all his scheme would be spoilt. There was but one way of doing it. Barbara must go and find Elizabeth. If they let Elizabeth into the secret she'd find a way of getting the plans back.

At first Barbara objected. She did not see why she should go alone. But Geoffrey persuaded her. Didn't she understand how desperately important it was? He looked so miserable that she gave in, and listened obediently to his instructions.

She was to go boldly up to the house and ask for Elizabeth. She could invent some excuse to see her alone. In the meanwhile he would go back to the Wheatsheaf and wait for her there.

But she caught him up even before he reached the wicketgate.

He turned round in astonishment to see her back so soon.

Breathless with running, she shook her head. It was no use. Elizabeth had gone out. Just as she came in sight of the house, the black coach drove by, going towards the gates. She could see Elizabeth and her grandmother inside it. So it was no use her going on.

They stared at one another helplessly. Suddenly Barbara had an idea. She seized Geoffrey's arm and pointed across the road to the inn. Look! There was Jenny, Mrs. Jarvis's daughter. She'd just arrived. Perhaps she had the afternoon off because my lady had gone out. She was such a nice girl. She might be able to help.

Geoffrey looked doubtful. It didn't seem very likely. But still, they had to do something. Barbara could try if she liked.

Without giving him a chance to change his mind, Barbara sped across the road.

She found Mrs. Jarvis and Jenny in the yard at the back of the house. They had seated themselves on a bench in the shade and were making fish-baskets; 'kiddles' Mrs. Jarvis called them, smiling at Barbara, and clearing a place for her to join the party. Had she ever seen a kiddle before? They were traps for catching fish. Surely she'd heard the saying 'a fine kiddle of fish'?

Baskets and Fish Kiddle

Barbara said 'Yes' politely. But she had not come to talk about fish traps and at the first opportunity she plunged into her story.

It sounded rather grand the way she put it. Geoffrey had fetched Father's plans from the cupboard to do some work on them. They had taken them into the Park, and Mad Margot had run away with them. They simply *must* have them back or they would get into most terrible trouble.

Mrs. Jarvis shook her head doubtfully. She didn't think they ought to have taken the plans out of doors. But still, she wouldn't like to see them get into trouble. Perhaps Jenny might be able to help. Madame Margot was very fond of Jenny.

She looked at her daughter hopefully.

Jenny said that she was willing to try. Of course she didn't

know anything about the plans. Madame Margot might have
given them to my lady, there was no telling. But she sometimes did take things for no reason at all, poor soul. If she had
them, she might be coaxed to give them up. Anyhow, there'd
be no harm in trying. When did Miss Barbara want them?
Should she go now?

Barbara said, 'Oh please,' with so much feeling that Mrs.
Jarvis smiled and told Jenny to be off. If she was lucky she
could be back in half an hour.

Thankfully Barbara went out to Geoffrey who heaved a great
sigh of relief. He took a seat upon the top of a gate opposite

Sitting on the gate

the inn and announced his intention of waiting there. It was
shady, and they would be able to see Jenny coming back.

But the half-hour passed, and then an hour, and then another
hour, and Jenny did not return. Twice Barbara crossed the
road to Mrs. Jarvis to make sure that they hadn't missed her.
But Mrs. Jarvis could only tell Barbara not to worry. She might
depend on it, if anyone could manage Mad Margot, Jenny
could—sooner or later.

So there was nothing to do but to be patient. It was not
easy. Geoffrey was beginning to talk desperately of going up
to the Hall himself, when they heard a shout behind them.

They both jumped down. The voice was familiar, and yet
they could not believe their ears.

Coming towards them across the road was Father.

For the moment, as she ran to meet him, Barbara forgot all about the plans. It was only afterwards, when the first excitement was over, that she remembered, and glanced back once more to see if Jenny was coming. But there was no one in sight.

Strolling back to the inn, while Father described how he had ridden down in six hours, with only one break, to give Silver a rest, Geoffrey and Barbara looked at one another anxiously. What would happen? Would Jenny walk in with the roll in her hand under Father's very nose? And would Mrs. Jarvis realize that it was a secret, or would she say the wrong thing? But as they went in, Mrs. Jarvis gave them a meaning smile, and they knew that anyway they were safe from that quarter.

While Jarvis was saying Good evening to Father, they got a chance to speak to each other. What was Geoffrey going to do? Barbara whispered. Wouldn't it be better to tell Father everything? He couldn't be very angry if he really understood.

But Geoffrey would not hear of it. He was distracted with worry and suspense. When Barbara tried to argue he lost his temper and told her it was all her fault anyway. If it hadn't been for her he would have gone back and fetched the plans before dinner.

As he turned on his heel and left her, Barbara burst into tears.

Mrs. Jarvis found her drying her eyes in the corner of the kitchen. Poor child, she was tired out with excitement. Was it the roll of papers that was the trouble? She must not worry. She'd send a messenger up to Jenny and find out what had happened. Barbara must cheer up now, or her Father would want to know what was the matter. Supper was almost ready.

Comforted, Barbara washed her face by the pump. Only one thought consoled her. Father could not look in the cupboard without their knowing of it, because Geoffrey had the key.

There was plenty to talk about at supper. Father brought all the news from the town. People in London were concerned about the war with France. King William was in Ireland fighting King James's party and most of the army was over there with him. In the meanwhile the French were cruising up and down the Channel, and we didn't seem able to stop them. In the City the Trained Bands were being mobilized, and he heard that in some parts of the country they had called up the Militia. He supposed that we should pull through somehow, but we always left everything to the last minute. However, it seemed to be peaceful enough down here.

Geoffrey shook his head. They were drilling the Militia here too. Mr. Lovegrove had told them so when they were walking up to the Hall.

Father caught him up quickly. To the Hall? Had they been up to the Hall, then?

Geoffrey said that they had. He told Father about their invitation, but he said so little about his own part in it that Barbara had to join in, and explain about his rescuing Elizabeth from the river.

Father was pleased. He said 'Good boy' several times. He wanted to know if there was any news about Sir Humphrey's return? No? Oh well, he hadn't expected any. He had only come this time just to see that the children were well and happy and to bring them a package from Aunt Anne. She was afraid that they might go short of clothes. He had a present for Geoffrey too—some paper and some coloured chalks, so that he could go on with his drawing.

At that moment Mrs. Jarvis came to clear the platters away. She made a sign to Barbara, and, picking up a dish, Barbara followed her out of the room.

It was all right, she whispered. Jenny had got the papers. Madame Margot had been difficult. She had only taken them out of curiosity. She did not know what they were, but she did not want to let them go, and it had needed hours of coaxing before she had allowed Jenny to have them.

Thankfully Barbara seized the roll and hid it in the folds of her skirt while she went to find Geoffrey.

Good luck was with her, for Father had gone out to the stable.

Geoffrey grabbed the plans and hurried upstairs to put them back in the cupboard.

With her heart suddenly lighter, Barbara turned to the parcel from Aunt Anne. There were two shirts for Geoffrey, also a new beaver hat and a pair of gloves with fringes, both of which he had been longing for. Barbara was glad. Perhaps they would help him to forget the misery of the last few hours. Her own dresses were of Holland, for every day. Mrs. Jarvis could put them in her wash-tub when they were dirty, wrote Aunt Anne.

She was so intent upon the new clothes that she did not notice that Father had come in and gone upstairs. Suddenly she heard his voice in the room above. What had happened? Had Geoffrey got the roll safely back into the cupboard, or had he been caught in the act? Surely, after all their trouble, it couldn't go wrong now.

In a few minutes Geoffrey came down. He beckoned to Barbara and she followed him outside.

The key had stuck again, he told her; just as it had done before. Father had come up and found him with the plans in his hand, and the key in the lock. He told Father that he had taken the plans out to study them. He'd been on the point of telling him about the site as well, but Father seized the roll and looked at it, and of course it had got a bit crumpled and dirty on the outside—nothing very much, but Father was very cross. Barbara knew what he was like when he was cross—he became cold and withering. He said that his plans weren't children's playthings. So of course it was no good trying to tell him anything.

Barbara nodded sympathetically. *She* knew. When Father got like that it was hopeless. Well? What happened next?

Then Father tried the key, and this time it turned quite easily. So he put the plans into the cupboard and the key into his own pocket and Geoffrey came downstairs. That was all.

Barbara sighed. Poor Geoffrey. It had all gone wrong. But she tried to console him. Anyway it was all right now, she said. The plans were safely back, and the house was not going to be started yet. There would be plenty of time to show Father the site when he was in a good mood again.

Geoffrey's new hat and gloves

Dinner in the kitchen

Chapter Fourteen

ACTUALLY Father seemed to have recovered his good humour by the next morning. He was up early and enjoying the sunshine outside when Barbara came downstairs.

He was going to the village this morning, he said. He wanted to see Ponting about the lock of the cupboard. It was sticking a bit. Would Barbara like to come with him? Geoffrey was buried in his books. When he heard that Father was going to ask Mr. Hayward for a report of his progress he seemed suddenly to remember that there were such things as Greek and Latin. So it would be best not to disturb him—Father chuckled to himself—no doubt the boy had a lot of lost time to make up.

Barbara skipped along happily. Certainly Father was in a good mood again. It might be possible to take him to the site this afternoon.

Mr. Ponting was in his workshop. There was no news about Ned. Father had not heard about the runaways, and he was obliged to listen to the story from the beginning. The two men shook their heads together over the dangers of the City for inexperienced boys, and Father told Barbara to go and play outside.

She wandered out into the village street and watched the people passing by. Two young women driving a stubborn donkey, its panniers full of vegetables for market, gave her plenty of amusement. Then a couple of children fetching home a batch of hot loaves from the bakehouse dropped the whole lot, chased them all over the road, wiped them clean with their dresses, and continued on their way. A gamekeeper passed, ignored and silent, with his two dogs at his heels and his matchlock over his shoulder. Finally a travelling tinker appeared, his packhorse labouring under a clattering load of pots and pans and kettles and gridirons. He was crying his trade, so that the women heard him and hurried out from the cottages.

In the midst of it all came Mrs. Hayward, carrying her covered basket.

She saw Barbara, and hastened to speak to her, scarcely waiting for her to complete her curtsey before she flooded her with a torrent of questions. There were so many things to

The stubborn donkey

find out about to-day. She had heard that Father had arrived from London. Did that mean that the new house was to begin at once? Barbara ought to know because apparently she had been up at the Hall. Was it true that Geoffrey had pulled little Elizabeth out of the river? Poor child. She was running for her life from that mad woman, they said.

So she went on, scarcely waiting for answers. When she had finished with their invitation to the Hall, she began about the visit of her Grace of Cleveland, to whom she referred as 'That woman'. She had the effrontery, Mrs. Hayward said with warmth, to bring that dreadful man 'Scum' Goodman in her train; a common highwayman he was, and ought to have been hanged.

This made Barbara open her eyes wide. A highwayman? Surely Mrs. Hayward did not mean the gallant who danced the

Mrs. Hayward dropped an elegant curtsey

coranto? He was a very fine gentleman. He could not possibly have been a highwayman.

Mrs. Hayward assured her that he had been—at one time—until he turned King's Evidence to save his skin. Cardonell Goodman his name was. *She* ought to know because she had known his father when she was young—a highly respectable parson. The son was educated at St. John's College, Cambridge, until he was expelled for defacing the Duke of Monmouth's portrait. Then he turned actor and highwayman; a most disgraceful young man.

Barbara was thrilled. It was he who had told her the story

about Claude Duval dancing the coranto with a lady on Hounslow Heath—and he was a highwayman himself all the time. She longed to get back to the inn to tell Geoffrey. If only Father would be quick.

At that very moment Father emerged from the joiner's shop. He bowed courteously to Mrs. Hayward who dropped an elegant curtsey. It was pleasant to see him in Ladybourne again, she said. He had been talking to Ponting? No doubt he had heard the dreadful story of those two boys running away to London.

Father said he was very sorry about it. London was no place for country lads, unless they had someone to look after them. He was concerned to hear that Geoffrey might have influenced Ned by his foolish chatter. Ponting said that they were always talking about London.

Mrs. Hayward shook her head gravely. Boys were very silly when they got together, and perhaps Ned and Geoffrey had seen rather too much of one another. She'd heard, on excellent authority, that Geoffrey had been with Ned and Dick Colman at the cock-fighting in Henley.

Father stared at her. At the cock-fighting? What did she mean?

Mrs. Hayward twittered nervously. Perhaps she shouldn't have mentioned it, she apologized. It came into her mind because it was at the cock-fight that those naughty boys won the money to go to London.

Father told her to go on. He wanted know to about it.

To Barbara's horror Mrs. Hayward produced the whole story. She had it, she said, from her friend Mrs. Brooksbank, the Rector's wife in Reading. Father perchance remembered them in their coach?

Father said he certainly remembered them. They had been very kind.

It was quite a coincidence, Mrs. Hayward continued. Mr. Brooksbank chanced to be in Henley that night, visiting an old parishioner who was living there. Riding past a low tavern on his way home he saw a crowd—in fact his way was barred by some sort of free fight. Among the faces in the crowd he recognized Ned Ponting and Geoffrey. He remembered Geoffrey at once, because Geoffrey had been so interested in his watch. He had thought him a most intelligent boy. He asked a man who was standing by what was going on, and the man told him that there had been a bout of cock-fighting; also that Ned and Geoffrey and the other boy with them, Dick Colman, had been gaming and had won a great deal of money. Mr. Brooksbank would have spoken to Geoffrey and taken him out of that crowd, but by the time he could move his horse, the boys had gone.

Father's face was like a thundercloud. He asked Mrs. Hayward how she had heard of it?

She had happened to visit Mrs. Brooksbank in Reading the next day, she replied quickly. Mrs. Brooksbank, of course, had it from her husband. She hoped that Father did not mind her mentioning it?

Father said that on the contrary it was right that he should know. He would speak to Geoffrey at once. Calling to Barbara, he turned back towards the Wheatsheaf.

Mrs. Hayward tripped beside them. It seemed that she could not leave the subject alone. Of course, she said, she did not blame Dick Colman quite so much. The boy was frantic to help his unfortunate mother, and no doubt he had been led astray by hopes of making money. But they had stolen a horse, and Farmer Whitgrave said he would hand them over to the law. It was all Ned Ponting's fault. It looked as if *he* would end up at Newgate, if not at the gallows.

Barbara caught her breath. The gallows! She had once seen the gibbet at Tyburn and she had never forgotten it.

At the Wheatsheaf Mrs. Hayward said Good day. She had enjoyed meeting them.

Father went into the parlour and sent Barbara to fetch Geoffrey. She was not to tell him why he was wanted. She was just to fetch him at once.

When they returned together, Father told them to shut the door. He had some questions to ask Geoffrey. Glancing at her brother's face, Barbara saw that it was very pale. Father began briskly, putting one question after the other without a pause.

Had Geoffrey helped in any way in Ned Ponting's plan for running off to London? No? Then had he known about it beforehand? No? Ponting was convinced that Geoffrey's stories about London had put the idea into Ned's mind. Was that true?

Geoffrey said he did not think so. Ned was always mad about London, long before they ever came here. Mrs. Jarvis would tell him that.

Barbara ventured to join in. Ned had got his stories about London from the bargemen on the top-path. Sam Pullet was a friend of his. Didn't Father remember Sam Pullet?—the horrible man with the black patch?

Father looked astonished. Yes, he remembered the fellow. So *he* was at the root of the trouble, was he? And had Geoffrey been consorting with Sam Pullet too?

Geoffrey shook his head. But Father continued to question him.

He had been told that Geoffrey had been frequenting cock-fights at a low tavern in Henley—and that he had been gaming and won a lot of money. What had Geoffrey to say to that?

There was a long pause. Geoffrey's face was flaming. At last he said that he had been once to a cock-fight—only just once—and he had lost his wager, not won it. Ned had won. So had Dick Colman. That is where they got the money to go to London.

There, it was out! Barbara felt almost relieved. She looked at Father's face to see how he had taken it.

Father looked sterner than ever. He spoke sharply.

If Geoffrey had lost all his money, would he please account for the four gold guineas which were at present in the pocket of his coat?

Clearly Geoffrey was taken aback. Father explained. As Geoffrey undressed last night he had, as usual, thrown his coat untidily across the stool. When Father came to bed later, he picked it up, and a guinea fell out. He felt in the pocket, and there were three more. Where did those guineas come from?

After a moment's hesitation Geoffrey said that he had won them at cards.

Father was withering. Cards and betting. Betting and cards. It seemed that he lost at one and gained on the other. What was the difference?

Geoffrey was near to tears. He said that he had won the money playing with her Grace of Cleveland when she was here. He could not help playing. It would have been rude to refuse.

Father did not comment on that. He seemed as if he had something more to say.

124

There was one other matter. He was very solemn. It was a very grave matter. He wanted Geoffrey to think well before he answered.

When he went back to London, he left the key of his cupboard in Geoffrey's charge. In that cupboard were his plans for the Great House. He knew that Geoffrey had been tampering with those. He caught him putting them back. But in the cupboard he had also left a purse containing five guineas. He had left it in case money should be needed for them while he was away. That purse had vanished. Could Geoffrey account for it?

Both Geoffrey and Barbara were genuinely astonished. There was no hesitation about Geoffrey's reply this time. He had never touched the purse.

Father looked at Barbara. Had she seen it? It was a small red purse of knitted silk. Aunt Anne made it. It contained five golden guineas.

Barbara knew the purse. Aunt Anne had given her a blue one like it. But she had not seen it.

Purse and guineas

What about the key? Father inquired. He had told Geoffrey to keep it always with him. Had he ever left it lying about?

Geoffrey declared quite definitely that he had never parted with the key. He wore it on a riband round his neck.

Father walked to the window. He stood staring out, deep in thought.

While his back was turned Barbara looked at Geoffrey and he at her. An idea had suddenly come into her mind and she could see that it had come to him too.

Ned! The night that the key had stuck Ned had opened the cupboard for them. It had been dark and she had held a light. Then the light had gone out. Ned would have had plenty of time to grab the purse. Barbara felt quite sick. What would Geoffrey do? Would he tell Father? What would happen to Ned if this came out? Mrs. Hayward had already talked about Newgate and the gallows.

Turning back into the room, Father asked one last question. Could Geoffrey then offer no suggestion as to where the purse had gone?

Geoffrey looked his father full in the face, and Barbara held her breath. Was he going to mention Ned?

But Geoffrey answered only 'No Sir'—then his voice shook a little.

'*I* didn't take it, Father,' he said simply.

For a long moment they stared at one another. Then Father sighed, and turned away.

Very well, he said. He must accept Geoffrey's word. But that did not alter the fact that Geoffrey was in serious disgrace. He had been mixed up with these boys who had stolen a horse

Pipes and rack

and run away from home. He had been cock-fighting and gaming at a low tavern. He had played cards for big stakes. To say that it would have been rude to refuse was no excuse. What would he have done, pray, if he had lost money instead of winning it? This was the beginning of the road that led to ruin. Perhaps it had been a mistake to leave them here alone. He had thought that they were old enough to be trusted. But apparently he had been wrong. Well—he would think it all over. Probably he would decide to take them back to London at once, where Geoffrey would be under proper discipline until he was apprenticed.

The rest of the day passed miserably. At dinner there were strangers present, two gentlemen riding from Oxford to London. The conversation was chiefly on the relative merits of tobacco from the Spanish Indies at nine or ten shillings a pound, and that which came from our own colony of Virginia and cost only half a crown. Pipes were produced and tobacco boxes exchanged. But to Barbara and Geoffrey Father addressed scarcely a word. Afterwards he went out. He was going to see Parson Hayward, he told Mrs. Jarvis. He would also go up to the Hall.

Left to themselves Geoffrey and Barbara went and sat on the river-bank. It might be their last afternoon, and by mutual consent they did not go near the site. They both felt that they could not bear it.

Barbara still wanted Geoffrey to talk to Father, and tell him about the site. If only he could persuade him to come and see it.

But Geoffrey was feeling quite hopeless. What was the use? he said miserably. Father would not listen to anything when he was angry like this. Certainly he'd never look at the site. No plan that he suggested would have a chance with Father now. He would just be taken back to London and apprenticed to a builder, without Oxford or Westminster or anything. And they'd pull down the old house and build the new one on the same piece of ground. Perhaps some day, after it was finished, they'd find *his* plan all laid out on the hill and then they'd be sorry.

He threw a stone savagely into the water and watched the eddies circle.

Barbara waited till it was calm again.

Father would get over it, she persisted. After all, he couldn't *really* believe that Geoffrey was a thief.

Father *did* believe it. It was no use her going on and on when it was as plain as a pikestaff what Father thought. He was under a cloud, and as he couldn't prove that he hadn't taken the purse, he'd just have to remain under it.

Barbara sighed deeply. It was awful. Perhaps after all they should tell Father about Ned.

Geoffrey said No very decidedly. They couldn't do that. He had fetched Ned himself and asked him to open the cupboard. He couldn't turn round now and give him away. After all, stealing a purse of money was a serious thing. He might go to prison for it.

Barbara nodded. Mrs. Hayward said that he would end up at Newgate. She'd even said the gallows.

Geoffrey looked startled. Well then, it was obvious that whatever happened they must not mention Ned. Besides, after all they didn't *know* that Ned had taken it.

Barbara said that he *must* have done. What else could have happened to it?

Geoffrey shrugged his shoulders. *He* didn't know. Perhaps Father hadn't left it there at all. He might have made a mistake, or dropped it, or anything.

Barbara could see that Geoffrey was only trying to excuse Ned. She sighed heavily, for though they had agreed to keep Ned out of it, she didn't know how it could ever be cleared up until Ned came home. Perhaps, when they got to London, Father could look for Sam Pullet, and find out what had become of him.

The Old House

Chapter Fifteen

BUT Father came in to supper with quite a different look on his face.

He had been to see Lady Ainsley, he told them. He was glad to say that she had taken a great fancy to them. She had actually invited them to stay at the Hall while he was away in London. He had gladly accepted her kindness for Barbara, but he felt that Geoffrey should be under the care of a man. Therefore he had asked Mr. Hayward, who had consented to take charge of him at the Parsonage. He would live there, but, at my lady's special request, he might go up to the Hall as often as he liked.

They were both tongue-tied with astonishment. After they had been expecting to be dragged back to London, this was an amazing contrast.

Barbara glanced at Geoffrey to see how he had taken it.

But apart from surprise he showed no emotion at all. Barbara asked how long they were to remain.

Father did not know. He supposed it would be until Sir Humphrey returned. Lady Ainsley had promised to send a message to London as soon as news arrived, so that he could come down at once. Then they would both join him at the Wheatsheaf again. So they need not pack up everything. They could leave behind anything they did not actually want. If they were ready early, he would see them safely settled before he left to-morrow.

He paused for a moment.

And he trusted, he added, in his former severe voice, that when he came again he would hear no more stories of gambling and disgrace. He hoped that a little time to think things over might bring a change of heart. It was never too late to repent, to confess, and to obtain forgiveness.

He looked at Geoffrey as he spoke. But Geoffrey did not answer. Only afterwards he said to Barbara rather bitterly that it was no good his saying that he hadn't taken the purse. Father just didn't believe him.

They both walked up to the Hall with Father in the morning. It was early. The dew still lay in a silver haze on the grass. Father wanted to get to horse and away, so Mrs. Jarvis had woken them before the sun was up, and helped Barbara to pack the few things she needed. She was only taking her two new holland dresses and the beloved blue embroidered one. Everything else could just remain at the Wheatsheaf. Mrs. Jarvis would keep her little room for her, she promised. No one else should use it until she returned.

Lady Ainsley was out in the garden when they arrived. She carried a basket and was gathering herbs for her still-room. Most plants were more potent if they were gathered in the pride of the morning before the dew had left them, she explained. Would Barbara like to help? She could have this little sharp prong and dig up daisy roots as Elizabeth was doing. Well washed and mixed with salt, they made an unfailing ease for a toothache, and it seemed, in her household, that somebody always had an aching tooth.

Obediently Barbara took the tool and she was already very busy when Father and Geoffrey said good-bye and left her.

Life at the Hall, Barbara discovered, was always busy. She had believed that great ladies, who lived in halls and castles, with lots of servants, spent their time resting or amusing themselves. Lady Ainsley, on the contrary, seemed never to rest. With her bunch of keys jangling from her waist, she was busy all through the day, from morning prayers in the hall, to the lighting of candles at night.

Ladybourne lived in a little world of its own, growing its own crops, grinding the corn at the mill, and making it into bread in its own bakehouse. It was not only the household, large as it was, that had to be provided for. When hard days came in the winter the whole village turned towards the Hall.

The village had first claim on all supplies before anything was sent to market. When pigs were killed or fat stock slaughtered, the village looked for its black puddings and its umble pies.

The summer months seemed to be one long bustle of preparation for winter. Fuel must be seen to, and wood was growing scarce. For so many centuries trees had been felled and burned extravagantly that now nothing must be cut without forethought and replanting. True that there was sea-coal from the river barges, but that was too dear to be used by any but the wealthy.

Then great joints of meat must be laid up in pickle. The sheltered fishponds must be stocked with live fish from the river. There were deer and pigs and rabbits and poultry and pigeons to care for, since they all helped with the problem of the many mouths to be fed. The brew-house produced ale from home-malted barley, and in the autumn there would be cider made in the home press.

This business of producing almost everything they needed was an astonishment to Barbara, who, in London, was accustomed to shops close at hand. She said so to Lady Ainsley one morning, as she followed her on her daily round of dairy and bakehouse and every corner where work went on.

But my lady only laughed at her. And where, pray, did she expect things to come from? From some fairyland across the seas? That was far too costly and too slow for anything but luxuries. If they did not provide themselves with food and firing they would pretty soon be hungry and cold.

Into this full life Barbara slipped easily and happily. All her days were spent with Elizabeth, and her nights too, since there was room for them both in Elizabeth's big bed. She was even privileged to use Elizabeth's most cherished possession, the little walnut desk which her father had given her before he went abroad. Barbara had always felt that it must be rather fun to have a sister, and now, to all intents and purposes, she had one.

But there was little time to play. Elizabeth was kept almost as busy as her grandmother, and whatever Elizabeth did, Barbara did too.

First of all there were lessons. Parson Hayward came twice a week, and for the rest there was Madame Margot. There were long hours over samplers, spent in learning to use their needles in every possible stitch. Then they must practise their music, either on the old virginals in Elizabeth's nursery or on the more elaborate harpsichord, with its two keyboards, in my lady's withdrawing room.

But when lessons and practising were finished the real work of the day had hardly begun. With big safeguards tied over their dresses, they learned to cook and to bake, to skim milk and make butter, to iron linen and fold it, to cut herbs and pound them. They made rose water and orange flower water, both for scent and for flavour; they preserved every fruit as it came into season, and, worst of all, they covered their heads with fine net and learned to tend bees.

There was a delicious drink made with honey. Elizabeth called it mead. Barbara, startled, said that Aunt Anne would

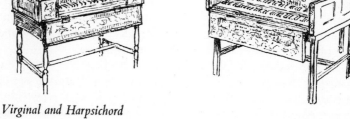

Virginal and Harpsichord

never allow her to taste mead. It was too intoxicating. Lady Ainsley smiled when Barbara quoted this. She said that Aunt Anne was quite right. True mead was powerful heady stuff. But this was mild enough. Really it was little more than barley water made with honey. Everybody drank it.

But even for the sake of the honey and the mead, Barbara did not think she would ever get used to bees. Elizabeth was not afraid of them, and Madame Margot had a strange power with them. She talked and crooned over them, and they crawled about her without ever stinging her. Secretly Barbara was terrified and the bees knew it. Whenever she came near, their buzzing seemed to grow more intense, and if she could she always seized an excuse to do some other task.

At first Barbara was ill at ease with Mad Margot. The Frenchwoman certainly was odd. She was given to moods.

Sometimes she scowled and was silent, hastening about her duties with her black veil pulled low over her face. At other times she was gay and full of fun, joining with her pupils in peals of laughter. There were days when she would suddenly pull Elizabeth on to her lap and rock her and call her 'Bébé', while Elizabeth's bright eyes twinkled at Barbara. Or she might have a black fit of jealousy, and storm and rave at them both for no better reason than that Elizabeth was happy in Barbara's company.

The old life at the Wheatsheaf seemed a long way off. Geoffrey came up to the Hall every afternoon, but they had little time alone together, and the site and their plan for the Great House was never mentioned. Sometimes Barbara wondered if he had forgotten it, but to forget was not like Geoffrey. And she was quite sure that he had not got over the trouble during Father's visit.

He still felt that he was under a cloud. There was a pre-occupation about him, and a faint air of bitterness which worried Barbara. She dared not break the silence and talk about it, and yet she felt that he was brooding. If only Ned would come home so that the mystery of the missing purse could be cleared up.

But two things gradually cheered him. First he was getting on well at the Parsonage. Mr. Hayward was a fine classical scholar, and when Geoffrey told him how he longed to go to Oxford, Mr. Hayward said 'Why not?' and talked of helping him to try for a scholarship. If he won one, perhaps Father might excuse him from his apprenticeship.

The second piece of happiness was Lady Ainsley's kindness. There was no doubt that she had taken a great liking to Geoffrey. She unlocked for him the door of Sir Humphrey's library, a large lofty room—the chapel of pre-Reformation days. It was an old library, she told him. Nowadays it was the fashion to have a library and people who cared nothing for scholarship were buying books which they never opened. Sir Humphrey was brought up to love his books and she was sure that Geoffrey would be careful with them.

Geoffrey flushed with pride. That, he confided to Barbara, was the way to treat a boy, instead of ordering and forbidding. All his spare time was spent in the library.

But Barbara, after one look at the shelves, and one sniff of the sweet musty smell of old leather, was off to the garden again.

133

Father did not write to Geoffrey after his return to London, but he wrote once to Mr. Hayward and said that he had not succeeded in tracing the waterman, Sam Pullet, and so of course there was no sign of Ned.

Except for this letter, little news came from the outer world. There were no visitors to bring tidings, and the News Letter, which should have arrived by the carrier, failed to turn up. But it did not seem to matter. Mr. Lovegrove heard news in Henley of the war. The French ships had beaten the combined English and Dutch fleets off Beachy Head—people said there was now nothing to stop the French from invading. The Militia must be drilled in real earnest. But even this danger seemed to make little stir in Ladybourne. The men-servants went off to hold parades now and then, but Lady Ainsley remained unmoved. Invasion or no invasion the lavender must be gathered and dried before it got too ripe, and if the blackcurrants were not picked and preserved there'd be no cordial for anybody's cold next winter.

One afternoon Mr. Hayward came up to the Hall with Geoffrey. He had been there in the morning for lessons, so clearly there must be something out of the ordinary to bring him back again.

Lady Ainsley was with Elizabeth and Barbara in the garden spreading armfuls of cut rosemary to dry in the sun. Parson Hayward, after offering his obedience, told her that he had come to bring her news of the missing lads, Ned Ponting and Dick Colman. He knew that she would wish to hear.

Barbara stood stock still. She could hardly bear the suspense.

Dick Colman had come home, Mr. Hayward began. He had been robbed in London of what little money he possessed. He had been beaten and half starved, and finally he had managed to tramp home again, begging his food on the way. Poor lad, he had learned a hard lesson.

'Poor lad, indeed,' Lady Ainsley agreed. And what about Ned Ponting? What had happened to him?

Mr. Hayward shook his head. He feared it would be a long time before Ned's home saw him again. The Press Gang had taken him.

Barbara gasped. The Press Gang! She really did not know what the Press Gang was, though she had often heard of it. She thought they were some sort of pirates. Oh, poor Ned! Perhaps he would be chained in a galley.

Parson Hayward was still talking. It was perfectly true apparently that the boys had gone off with the man, Sam Pullet, but luckily the Press Gang had taken him too. So he would be kept out of mischief, and wouldn't be enticing any more honest lads from their homes.

Lady Ainsley, looking very grave, inquired how Ned's mother had received the news?

Mr. Hayward said that she had not heard it yet. Ponting was not in his workshop when he called there half an hour since. He was on his way now to find him down at the mill and break it to him.

Lady Ainsley agreed that he must go at once. She herself would go and see the boy's mother.

Geoffrey, it seemed, was going to the mill with Mr. Hayward. Finding that no one was paying any attention to her, Barbara fell into step beside him. They were half-way across the Park before Mr. Hayward noticed her. When he did, he only smiled and did not send her back. It was on the tip of her tongue to ask him what the Press Gang was, but she thought that Geoffrey would laugh at her. It would be better to stay quiet. She'd be sure to learn something about it when they began to talk.

She remained outside with Geoffrey while Mr. Hayward went into the mill to find Ponting. The mill-wheel was not working. It was very quiet. A kingfisher flashed like a bright jewel across the stream. A little way off a fish jumped. In the distance they could hear the steady murmur of water splashing over the weir.

Barbara sighed a little. Poor Ned. They were bound to think of Ned whenever they came near the river. How she wished he could come home, with his grin and his freckles and his exciting chatter. Then, too, the business of the purse might be solved, though it was almost as impossible to believe that he had taken it, as it was to suspect Geoffrey.

They leaned over the hand-rail of the little bridge in silence. Presently Mr. Hayward came out, followed by Ponting and his brother, the miller, in his floury smock. They lingered talking a minute more, then with a nod the miller went back to his work and the parson and Ponting crossed the bridge.

Ponting did not look as upset as they had expected. On the contrary he greeted Geoffrey quite cheerfully and asked if he had heard the news. That young rascal had over-reached himself this time.

Geoffrey wanted to speak to Ponting. That was why he had come. He was anxious to make Ned's father understand that he had really done nothing to encourage Ned to run away. He had not the slightest idea that Ned was planning to go.

Ponting was pleased. It was good of Master Geoffrey to speak that way. Maybe in the first shock hard things had been said. But as a matter of fact he'd never really blamed Geoffrey. Ned was full of wild ideas. What had happened might be the best thing for him. He'd far rather think of the boy in the King's ships than in Newgate jail. He wanted to see the world and he'd see it now with a vengeance. A little discipline was what he needed, even if he got it across his back with a knotted rope, as they did in the Navy.

The Navy? That did not sound like pirates. Barbara glanced, puzzled, from one to the other. As they crossed the Park she got a chance to ask Mr. Hayward. Please, what was the Press Gang that had taken Ned? Were they pirates?

Pirates? Mr. Hayward laughed. No! It wasn't as bad as that. They were King's men collecting crews for the ships of the King's Navy. Going to sea was a hard life and it was difficult to man the ships, so—like that story in the Bible—they'd got an order from the King, to compel them to come in. The Press Gang raided the taverns and the river quays, and seized any likely men or lads they found—whether they wanted to go or not. Often the men had wives and families, and in that case it was a great hardship. But in Ned's case he agreed that it was probably quite a good thing—though he doubted whether the lad's mother would look upon it in that light.

Barbara was much relieved. At any rate she would not have to think of Ned being sold as a slave. But she asked one more important question. How long would it be before he came home?

Parson Hayward could not say. Certainly he would not come for a very long time.

In bed that night Barbara lay thinking.

If Ned did not come back no one would ever know the truth about that purse, and Father would just go on believing that Geoffrey had taken it.

What ought she to do? If she asked Geoffrey he certainly would not let her clear him by putting the blame upon Ned, and if she asked any grown-up person like Mr. Hayward, or Lady Ainsley or even Aunt Anne, it would come to exactly the same thing as if she told Father right out. Oh, if only she knew what to do. If only she had someone with whom she could talk it over.

It was very hot in the big bed, which was deep with feathers and stuffy behind its embroidered hangings. Beside her Elizabeth lay in a restless sleep. She had tossed her share of the bed-clothes over to Barbara's side of the bed, and to rid herself of them, Barbara slid to the floor.

The moon shone brightly through the little diamond panes.

The King's Ships

She tiptoed to the windows. She knew that night winds were dangerous, but she was so hot that she could hardly breathe. Greatly daring she unlatched the casement and peeped out.

A wave of warm sweet air greeted her. How lovely it was —not a bit cold. The roses under the window were like big white rosettes, although by daylight they were pink. She leaned right out deep in vague thoughts about nothing in particular, and listening to sounds that seemed to come from far away—a moorhen down by the river, owls in the trees of the Park.

Suddenly something darted close by her head. It startled her. A bat! Ugh! She shut the window so hastily that Elizabeth woke and called her name in a frightened undertone. Where was she? What was she doing over there?

Barbara scrambled back into bed. She explained that she had been so hot that she had opened the window.

They lay back on the pillows talking

By this time Elizabeth was wide awake too, and she in her turn was, she said, roasted alive. They pushed off some of the bedclothes and lay back on the pillows talking softly.

Suddenly it came to Barbara that here was the one person to whom she might tell all her trouble. She and Elizabeth had weeks ago exchanged vows of eternal friendship. If Elizabeth spit on her finger and crossed her throat, and swore secrecy, surely there would be no harm in telling her. Barbara decided to risk it.

The story was rather complicated, because she began at the wrong end. But Elizabeth was thrilled. She asked question after question until she got it all clear. The part about Geoffrey losing his money at the cock-fighting, and winning it back by playing cards with her Grace of Cleveland was just like a story-book, she said; and she thought it was splendid of him not to tell Father about the cupboard, for fear of giving Ned away. But she couldn't understand why they wanted the plans so badly that they had to get Ned to unlock the door. What did they want them for?

Barbara hesitated for just a moment longer. To answer that question meant telling her about the site. But now that she had told so much, she couldn't very well stop. And after all Elizabeth *had* spit and crossed her throat.

So she told her everything: how they had found the place in the Park, and how Geoffrey had decided that it was a wonderful site for the new house; how they had pegged it out, and marked it with stones; how Margot had taken the plans, and Jenny had got them again; right up to the point where Father had caught Geoffrey putting them back in the cupboard, which was where she had begun.

Elizabeth could scarcely control her excitement. She bounced up and down on the feather bed. Oh lovely, lovely, she cried. And was the house still there, under the leaves? Would Barbara take her to see it?

Barbara said Yes. There wasn't any-thing else she could say. After all, now that Elizabeth knew all about it, she might as well see it—so long as she didn't tell anyone—not even Geoffrey.

Elizabeth was still jumping about when suddenly the door opened. Lady Ainsley stood in the entrance, in her night-gown, a flickering taper in her hand.

Taper holder

What was all this about? she asked sternly. Did they not know that it was past midnight? Why weren't they asleep this long time instead of romping as if it were midday?

Instantly they became as quiet as mice. For one awful moment Barbara was afraid that Elizabeth might explain too much. But Elizabeth only said in a meek little voice that they could not sleep. They were so dreadfully hot.

Her grandmother was sympathetic. She stuck her taper into a holder and came across to look at the tumbled bed.

Poor children, she said compassionately. They could get out of bed and remake it, Elizabeth on one side and Barbara on the other. See! She would help them shake up the feathers, and then they could put the clothes smoothly back, while she went and fetched them a drink of cold milk. No, not like that; *smoothly!* Such big girls, and not yet able to make a bed properly! Now, leave it open to get cool. Had they both said their prayers last night? Very well then, it wouldn't hurt them to say another. Elizabeth could say her favourite psalm—'The Lord is my Shepherd.'

Kneeling in the moonlight Barbara felt suddenly calm. She no longer wanted to chatter.

They drank their milk before they got back into bed. It was cooler now. Lady Ainsley laid the cover lightly over them and told them to count sheep going through a gate.

Counting sheep was just right. It all fitted with the psalm. The sheep and the gate faded into green pastures and still waters, and Barbara slept.

Elizabeth's desk

The mulberry tree

Chapter Sixteen

SHE was rather afraid of what Geoffrey would say when he found out that she had told Elizabeth about the site. Several times she screwed up her courage to confess to him, but she never succeeded in bringing herself to the point. It was easy to assure herself that Geoffrey would not mind. After all, on that afternoon when the plans were stolen, it was he who had suggested letting Elizabeth into the secret. But somehow it was different now. So she went on putting it off from day to day.

In the meanwhile, Elizabeth gave her no peace about going to see the site.

As Geoffrey had not been told, it was important to choose a time when he would not be likely to appear. Therefore on a morning when he had ridden to Henley with Parson Hayward, she told Elizabeth that she would take her.

It seemed strange to go to the site from the Hall instead of from their old wicket-gate, but she found the way without any difficulty. Some of the leaves had drifted, and here and there rows of little white stones showed through. But in other places weeds had grown up and the pattern was lost in a veil of young green. Barbara set to work to clear it, and as soon as she learned how, Elizabeth helped her. Before long the plan of the Great House stood out as clearly as ever.

Elizabeth danced about with excitement. What fun!

What fun! Why, it was like a real building. They could play houses in it perfectly. Which was the front door? She would be the mistress and Barbara could drive up to visit her.

This was just what Barbara had always secretly longed to do. But with Geoffrey she had never dared. He would have felt that she was turning his beloved site into a nursery game.

But now she could play to her heart's content. She swept up the make-believe drive in her make-believe coach to where Elizabeth stood at the top of the make-believe steps, to receive her with full ceremony. Then they paraded through the house, from room to room, though the game got a little mixed up when Barbara, the guest, had to show Elizabeth, the hostess, which way to go.

The pump

They were standing on the future terrace admiring the view when the dinner bell at the Hall rang in the distance. 'Run,' cried Elizabeth. They could leave the plan just as it was for a time. No one was likely to come.

They picked up their skirts and scampered across the Park. They arrived so hot and dishevelled that they dared not go in like that. The pump in the yard was the nearest, Elizabeth cried. There was a towel hanging on the dairy door.

A quick dab with cold water had to be enough, and each of them smoothed the other's head with wet hands to make it look brushed.

Such makeshifts did not deceive Lady Ainsley and even their best curtsies and their prayers for pardon did not save them from a scolding. Where had they been? she inquired. Elizabeth answered simply 'In the park,' and Barbara was glad that Geoffrey wasn't there to see her hot cheeks and ask awkward questions.

But Geoffrey was not in a mood to notice anything when

he arrived at the Hall that afternoon. He was just brimming over with excitement.

Mr. Hayward was riding up to Oxford to attend a meeting at his old college. He was going to stay there for two nights, and he had invited Geoffrey to go with him. They were starting early on the morrow.

To Geoffrey it was a sort of pilgrimage—his first visit to Oxford. Mr. Hayward had promised to take him round and show him everything. And while Mr. Hayward was at his meeting he could go out by himself.

He'd made up his mind already that he would go first to see Sir Christopher's new tower at Christchurch; someone had nicknamed it Tom Tower after its big bell. Then he'd see Wadham, Sir Christopher's old college, where he had been a commoner. In fact he might see his actual rooms. He knew just where they were. Sir Christopher himself had told him lots of stories about his boyhood, when he was smoking his pipe after dinner with Father in London. Didn't Barbara remember? No, of course she didn't. She'd gone to bed.

Barbara, stung into retort, reminded him that it had been after his bedtime too. He'd only been allowed to sit up because Sir Christopher was coming.

Geoffrey brushed the interruption aside.

If he ever went to Oxford, he'd like to go to Wadham too. But Mr. Hayward said he wouldn't have much chance, for Wadham was mostly for West Country boys. The Wrens came from Wiltshire. That was why Sir Christopher went there.

He rambled on and on, lying on his back in the garden under the shade of the Mulberry Tree—called 'King James's tree,' because King James the First had planted it himself, at the time that he wanted everybody to keep silkworms. Elizabeth and Barbara were plaiting straw to make shady hats for themselves, and Elizabeth thought that Geoffrey

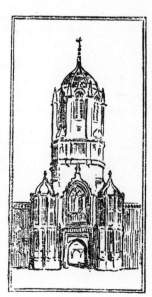

Tom Tower, Oxford

143

might help instead of just gazing up into the tree and talking. But Barbara whispered to her to leave him alone. If he was talking about Oxford, she wouldn't have to tell him about the site just yet.

Lady Ainsley came out presently, and then Geoffrey had to stop and jump to his feet. But he started again almost at once, because of course she had to be told about his journey to Oxford.

She was delighted. He worked so hard, she said, that he deserved an outing. She gave him a commission to do for her in Oxford, and he went off with something of the old swagger which Barbara had not seen since the days in London when he used to go out with Father.

During the few days that Geoffrey was away Barbara and Elizabeth paid several visits to the site, for the absence of Mr. Hayward from lessons gave them a little more spare time. Elizabeth never tired of playing houses, and she was quite annoyed at the end when Barbara insisted on putting the leaves back over the plan. Nobody ever came that way, she declared. It was just stupid to hide it. After all it wouldn't really matter if anyone did see it.

Barbara retorted in a hurry by reminding Elizabeth that it was a secret. Didn't she remember that it was a secret? She had promised. It was Geoffrey's secret, and he wanted it kept covered up.

She made up her mind that she really must tell Geoffrey that she had taken Elizabeth there. She couldn't help it if he was angry. At the very first chance she must tell him.

When Geoffrey arrived back, he was so bubbling over with excitement about all he had seen in Oxford that she could not get a word in. She went to bed the first night after his return vowing to herself that whatever happened she would tell him in the morning.

But the next morning he came in unusually early, while she and Elizabeth were sitting on the settee working their daily hour on their samplers. One glance at his face was enough to show her that the thing she dreaded had happened. He had found out.

He was so angry that he attacked her at once, even though it was in front of Elizabeth.

Had she been to the site? he demanded. He'd just been

down to have a look at it, and all the leaves were tossed about
anyhow. Was it her doing or had someone else found it out?

Feeling suddenly as if it was Father questioning her, Barbara
told him the truth. But she was careful not to say too much
about playing houses.

Before Geoffrey could reply, Elizabeth joined in. She'd
been there with Barbara, she said. She thought it was wonderful, and the house was absolutely lovely—just like a real one.
She couldn't think how he had done it all.

Geoffrey's frown faded. Did she really like it? he questioned,
quite eagerly. Didn't she think it was a lovely place for a
house? Of course it was a secret. She understood that,
didn't she? He'd got to show it to Father first, before anyone
else knew.

Elizabeth nodded. Oh, yes, she understood. But, whatever
happened, the new house simply *must* be built there, and then
this one wouldn't have to be pulled down. Grandmother
would be happy about that. What would the new house look
like? Would it be like this one?

Geoffrey pulled from his pocket a crumpled copy of the
London Mercury which he had brought from Oxford, and
began to scribble in the margin with a little stump of chalk.
He wished he could show her the picture he'd drawn of it, he
said. Barbara had seen it. But he'd torn it up that day when
he thought they were going back to London. He'd do another
if he had the paper and things. Father had brought him some
from London but he'd finished it all. Anyhow, perhaps she
could get an idea from this.

He pushed the news sheet towards her. Elizabeth peered
at the tiny drawing, and shook her head. It was too small,
she said. Did he really mean that he wanted drawing things?
Because she knew where there were plenty.

Geoffrey eagerly said Yes. He badly wanted to do another
picture of the house before Father came again. And Barbara
joined in to explain how good Geoffrey was at drawing. Father
said he'd be good enough to be a real artist if he wasn't going to
be an architect.

Elizabeth put down her sewing things, shook out her skirts
and told them to follow her.

She led the way downstairs, and across the hall to the library
wing. Closing the door after them, with an air of mystery,

she crossed to a dark corner of the room and opened a little door in the panelling. Geoffrey stared at it in astonishment. All the time that he had been working there, he exclaimed, he had never realized that the panelling would open.

A narrow staircase lay behind the panel. Elizabeth went up first.

The stairs rose into a lofty room, open to the rafters, its walls draped with faded hangings and lighted by one big window. Geoffrey gazed up at the beams overhead. Of course, he said, more to himself than to them: the library was made from the old chapel. This was the upper part, cut off when they built the ceiling. But why on earth hadn't he noticed that window? It must look out on to the kitchen court.

He started to cross to see for himself when suddenly he noticed the contents of the room, and stood still in amazement.

It was unfurnished except for a large table, a couple of stools and a plain oak cupboard. But on the table lay a litter of artist's materials—glass jars filled with brilliant powdered colours, flasks of oil and varnish, a collection of crayons, chalks, paintbrushes, and a great untidy pile of paper, all covered thick with dust.

Beyond the table stood an easel, with a picture on it draped entirely in a plain cover of dark cloth.

Geoffrey halted by the table lifting first one thing and then another as if in a dream. Why, there was everything here, he exclaimed. Absolutely everything! How on earth did it get here? Was it some artist's studio? Might he use them? Did Elizabeth mean that he could use them?

Elizabeth said Yes, excited by the effect she had produced. Of course he could use them. Her grandmother had told him that he could use the library. And this was, in a sort of way, part of the library. No one ever came up here. So he could do what he liked without being disturbed. They were oil paints, weren't they? Did he know how to use oil paints?

Geoffrey nodded. Yes, he'd had some lessons. Of course he'd not done very much, but he'd love to try. He picked up a big palette, blew the dust from it, and balanced it on his arm.

Barbara went round to the other side of the table, and stood

146

in front of the easel. What was under the cover? she asked Elizabeth.

After a second's hesitation Elizabeth tiptoed softly to the easel, almost as if someone might hear her. She pulled the cover away.

Beneath it, on an un-framed canvas, was the picture of a lady in red. Clearly it was unfinished, for though the head and the hands were lifelike, the dress was only just suggested.

Painting things

'Who is it?' whispered Barbara. But there was no need for her to ask. The dark hair and eyes, and the elfish tilt of the eye-brows were unmistakable. The answer was obvious long before Elizabeth replied 'My mother'.

Geoffrey laid down the palette and came to gaze too. Barbara remembered the story that Father had told them about a painter who had brought the sickness from London when he came to do the portrait of Sir Humphrey's first wife. Was this the very picture? she asked.

Elizabeth nodded. Yes, this was the one. She was only a baby when her mother died, so of course she did not remember anything about it. But her father would never come up here any more. That was why everything had been left just as it was. It was a lovely picture. It seemed a pity that it had never been finished.

They all gazed in silence for some moments. At last Geoffrey turned back and began cleaning the dust and cobwebs from a pile of paint-brushes, sorting the chalks and the paper, and clearing a space on the table. Then he pulled up a stool and sat down.

For a few minutes they watched him. But his drawing seemed to be all straight lines and measurements, so in a whisper Elizabeth suggested to Barbara that they should leave him.

There was that music that Mr. Hayward had brought them from Oxford—*Dr. Blow's Lessons for the Harpsichord*—they hadn't tried it yet.

After that Geoffrey went into the library every afternoon when he arrived from the Parsonage, and Elizabeth and Barbara, exchanging glances, guessed that he had vanished upstairs to the painting-room. But they did not follow him. When the first excitement had died down, they found the painting-room both dusty and dull. There were far more interesting things going on outside. Haymaking had begun and there was plenty of fun in the hayfields where all the village turned up to help with the turning and tossing, and my lady sent out cakes and ale for all. The only person missing was Geoffrey, but no one noticed his absence, though my lady remarked that he was very attentive to his books. Barbara saw him once, vanishing between the trees in the direction of the site, but he carried a drawing-board under his arm, and she knew that he did not want to be noticed.

The haysel lasted more than a week, but when it was all over Barbara and Elizabeth thought that they might as well see what he had been doing.

They chose a morning when everyone was out of the way. The Militia were being paraded in Henley for an inspection by the King's officer. Mr. Hayward had gone as chaplain and every man from the Hall was called upon to attend, so that the place seemed still and quiet, like a Sunday.

The maid-servants were all busy in the kitchen or the buttery; old Giles the butler, the only man left in the house, had led my lady away for an inspection of the brew-house, and Mistress Margot had taken a batch of fresh spun flax thread to the village to be woven into linen cloth on some of the cottage looms. So when they closed the library door behind them, opened the panel and crept up the narrow stairs, they seemed unlikely to be disturbed.

Geoffrey was already at work, pounding colour with pestle and mortar. He had, apparently, cleaned and tidied the table thoroughly. The brushes were stuck neatly, head up, into an empty jar; the papers were sorted and stacked, the palette had been used, and there was a delicious smell of fresh oil paint.

He seemed quite glad to see them, and eager to show off what he had been doing. First there were drawings of the new house, very like the one which Barbara had seen at the Wheat-

sheaf. Elizabeth thought they were dreadfully dull, and Barbara, this time eager to defend Geoffrey, explained that all
architects' drawings were like that. Father's were duller still.

But this time Geoffrey did not seem to mind his picture
being called dull. He'd done another, he said. He'd tried it
in oil, just to show what the house would look like when it
was finished. And he'd been down to the river and painted it on
the spot. It wasn't very good, but he was going to try it again.

He produced a small canvas and propped it on the table.
It was all there quite plainly—the river, and the hill with all the
trees, and the new house standing on the hill, not nearly so ugly
as it was in the drawing.

Barbara and Elizabeth thought it was a lovely picture.
Elizabeth looked at Geoffrey quite with awe, and even Barbara
said she did not know he could paint as well as that. It was
much, much better than the things he had painted in London.

Geoffrey was delighted with their praise. It wasn't quite
finished, he said. He'd just been mixing up a little more colour.
He wanted to get it done this morning.

He scooped the colour on to the palette, took up his brushes
and got to work, the frown of concentration on his brow which
Barbara knew of old.

They watched him for a while. Then Elizabeth grew bored
and began to wander about the room. There was silence for
a few moments. At last Barbara heard Elizabeth call her.

For a moment she wondered where Elizabeth had gone.
Then she noticed that the tall oak press was standing open, and
the voice came from behind its door. She went to have a look.

Elizabeth was lifting down a dress from the cupboard. It
was a red dress, of heavy glinting satin. Barbara recognized
the colour at once. It was the red dress of the portrait.

Elizabeth's eyes were shining with excitement. She'd got
an idea, she cried. Geoffrey could paint. Why couldn't he
finish the picture? Why not finish the painting of the dress?

Barbara, feeling suddenly chilly and frightened, looked
round to see what Geoffrey would say. He wouldn't, oh
surely he wouldn't touch the picture. But Geoffrey, palette in
hand, was still engrossed in his work.

Shrilly, Elizabeth called him again, and this time he glanced
round. Barbara saw a look of startled horror spring to his
face, and, following his eyes, she turned towards Elizabeth again.

But Elizabeth had vanished completely in the voluminous folds of the red satin. Just at that moment her head emerged through the top of the dress. It was much too big for her, but the fullness was supported in part by her own skirts underneath. When she stretched herself on tiptoe so that the creases straightened a little, laughing to see the effect, the likeness to the portrait was so striking that both Barbara and Geoffrey exclaimed aloud.

Elizabeth bounced up and down in the dress, brimming over with excitement.

'Finish the picture,' she called to Geoffrey. 'Oh do! do! Finish the picture.'

Horrified Geoffrey shook his head. He wouldn't touch it. He wouldn't dare.

Only the dress, Elizabeth persisted. There was only the dress to finish.

She stamped her foot to make him do it.

Just at that moment, behind them a cry rang out.

They all turned, startled.

At the top of the stairs, her hands wrung together, her eyes wild and staring, stood Mad Margot.

Suddenly she sprang at Elizabeth, clutching her, shaking her, tearing at the red dress, while Elizabeth, terrified, cried 'No! No! No!' at the top of her voice.

Geoffrey and Barbara darted to the rescue, trying to drag those clinging hands away from Elizabeth. For what seemed an age they struggled, the poor demented woman gripping madly, the frightened child screaming.

Then all at once she relaxed and let Elizabeth go, dropped to the floor and sat there, crying and sobbing and rocking herself to and fro.

Elizabeth checked her own tears, and she and Barbara stroked and coaxed and soothed while Geoffrey looked helplessly on. But the more they petted the louder Margot sobbed.

Barbara had just called to Geoffrey to go for help, when a footstep sounded on the stairs. It was Lady Ainsley.

Barely looking round she seemed at a glance to take in what was happening. The first sound of her voice, the first touch of her hand, and she commanded the situation. Margot's cries grew fewer, her sobs quieter. Soon she was on her feet, and between Lady Ainsley and Elizabeth, now out of the red dress, she was persuaded to go down the stairs.

Fire!

Chapter Seventeen

LEFT alone Barbara and Geoffrey stared at one another across the remains of the crushéd red dress and the scattered brushes and palette. Barbara was shaken with the shock of that dreadful scene, but Geoffrey was whiter still. He kept saying softly, 'Horrible, horrible.'

Barbara agreed with him. But it really wasn't their fault. They had not been doing anything wrong. Did he think my lady was very angry?

Had she not noticed my lady's face? Geoffrey replied. When she looked at him, she had made him feel completely ashamed. He had realized quite suddenly that they ought not to be up here at all. And then to be caught like this, with the palette in his hand. It was horrible.

Again Barbara said that it wasn't their fault. Elizabeth had brought them here. She had never said that they ought not to come. Did he think my lady would come back?

They waited in silence, Geoffrey gazing blankly out of the window, Barbara wondering whether she ought to pick up the red dress and hang it back in the press.

At last, after she had done so, Geoffrey turned. He was going down to find my lady, he said. He just couldn't stand this.

He led the way down the narrow stairs.

It was all quiet below. The library was empty, so they

turned out of the chapel wing, through the passage and into the hall.

To their astonishment, there sat my lady, all alone and quietly spinning, just exactly as she had been sitting the first day that they came.

Geoffrey went straight up to her, his white face suddenly very red.

He wanted to ask pardon, he said, for being in the painting-room without her permission. He had used the paints and the palette, and the other things, but he had not touched the picture. He wanted her to know that. He had not thought of touching it. He hoped that she would forgive him.

Lady Ainsley stopped the whirr of her wheel while he made his speech. Then she said very gently that she did not blame him. He could not know that the room was set apart. Besides, she would have allowed him in any case, though she would not have allowed Elizabeth to turn it into a playroom. It was Elizabeth whom she blamed. Elizabeth was vain and heartless, decking herself out in her dead mother's dress. She looked so like her mother, the little jade, that poor Margot was nearly crazed with the shock.

There was a pause, and Barbara dared to ask if Madame Margot was mending.

Lady Ainsley said she was resting on the day-bed in the parlour. A draught from the still-room had soothed her, and she hoped that she would sleep. As for Elizabeth she had sent her to bed. She needed a little solitude to repent of her vanity.

Then she looked at them both. They had best get something to do to occupy them, she said. For herself, when she felt overburdened, she always went to her spinning-wheel. It was of all occupations the most soothing. She must teach Barbara to spin; but then what about Geoffrey? She smiled at him. Would Geoffrey show her the drawings he had been doing?

Geoffrey looked embarrassed. He would like to show them, he said. But he would have to explain—my lady did not know——

Lady Ainsley interrupted.

My lady did know, she said. They were drawings of his new plan, were they not?

Day-bed

Barbara drew a quick breath, and Geoffrey looked at her in astonishment.

She knew about all his plan, she told him. And all about the new site too. Elizabeth had told her. They did not know Elizabeth very well, if they had not yet realized that she was a child who could not keep a secret.

For some moments there was silence, and then, as Lady Ainsley asked him again, Geoffrey fetched the drawings and spread them on the table on the dais.

At first Lady Ainsley was a little puzzled by them. But when she saw the picture of the site from the river, she sat for a long time with it in her hand. Then she said that she would like to see the site. It was a fine day and not too hot. She would find out if Margot was asleep. If so they might go now.

It was as though a great weight had been lifted from Geoffrey's mind. When they reached the grove of trees, Lady Ainsley paused to look round her. Certainly it was a lovely spot, she remarked. She had never realized before that the view was so beautiful.

The plan itself was covered with leaves and none of it was visible from where they stood. But Geoffrey and Barbara darted down and worked furiously, brushing and scooping, until, bit by bit, the design appeared.

Lady Ainsley was amazed. It was wonderful, she declared. They must have worked very hard and very neatly to have got it so exact. She was impressed with all the detail, showing where the doors and windows would come. The little white stones —that was a brilliant idea; and Barbara was filled with delight when Geoffrey said that it was she who had thought of that part.

Geoffrey spread the drawings on the table

They lingered for a long time. Lady Ainsley made a tour of the new house almost as carefully as if the walls were actually standing. To Geoffrey's joy she invited him to show her round.

The entrance to the house would lie on the side furthest from the river and she would approach it, he told her, by a big sweeping drive. Up the steps and under the porch she would reach the hall—not a dining-hall like the one at the old house, but a big entrance hall in the modern manner. The grand staircase went up from that and opened on to a gallery. Across the hall, opposite the front door, lay the great parlour, which was a long room with big windows, facing towards the river. Here he had made the only difference from Father's plan; he had designed a central door with a flight of steps, just like the entrance on the other side of the house, opening upon the terrace gardens with the wonderful view.

Alongside the parlour lay the withdrawing rooms, the dining-room and a fine library. There were the kitchens and the servants' quarters and the stables, all beyond that. Upstairs there would be bedrooms, and, most astonishing of all, a bathing-room with a bath of marble, and water-cocks, one for hot water and one for cold. But of course he could not take her upstairs because really it was only a ground plan.

They all laughed at that; and Geoffrey added, since he was afraid that he was getting too much credit, that the house itself was all Father's. He really had done nothing to the design except to fit it on to the new site.

Lady Ainsley nodded. She understood that. But all the same it was very remarkable. Of course, she pointed out, it was not her house. It was being built for future generations. She had been mistress of the old Hall, the one they knew and loved. No grand new mansion, however fine it was, could be home to her. But young people must choose for themselves. And anyway she would promise Geoffrey that his site should be considered.

It was the day of Geoffrey's life. He opened his heart as they strolled back, and all his hopes and ambitions came rushing out; architecture, Sir Christopher, Oxford—all mixed up together. Never had Barbara heard him talk like this.

Lady Ainsley listened and encouraged him. He was right to set his aims high, she told him. If he made up his mind that he would never be satisfied with second best, she believed that he would succeed.

As they approached it the old Hall seemed to look more beautiful than ever in the light of the afternoon sun.

Lady Ainsley fixed her eyes on it with a gaze full of love and sadness. Why, oh why, did anyone want to build another house? thought Barbara.

They turned the corner of the kitchen court to go in by

the side door. Lady Ainsley halted abruptly, her face suddenly ashen.

'Look!' she cried. 'Fire!'

She pointed across the courtyard towards the chapel wing. From the open window of the painting-room smoke poured out. Worse—behind it, through the clouded panes of the window-glass they could see an ominous flickering light.

The painting-room was on fire.

At Lady Ainsley's cry the servants came running out—women, women, nothing but women, with the sole exception of old Giles, trying to run as fast as his rheumatic limbs would let him. With them came Elizabeth, her eyes wide with horror. Barbara realized that all the men were away, at the Militia Parade.

Everything suddenly became turmoil. Lady Ainsley stood in the middle of the court issuing orders in a voice that rang out even above the servants' babble.

Already Jenny Jarvis was working at the pump-handle for dear life. Barbara rushed into the dairy and seizing two milking buckets ran back with them to the pump. Suddenly the sound of crashing glass startled her. She turned and looked up at the burning room.

There stood Geoffrey, knocking out the window with a wooden stool. The diamond panes were flying, smashed to fragments, releasing fresh clouds of smoke. Horrified, Barbara clapped her hands over her mouth. What was he doing? He would be killed.

Geoffrey was throwing out of the window piles of papers and drawings, scorched and smouldering, the palette and paints, bottles and jars of oils and varnishes. After them came the canvas itself, smoked and blackened. Then he vanished back into the room.

Old Giles hurried into the house by the library door, and Lady Ainsley followed. Nearly crazy with fear for Geoffrey, Barbara rushed after her.

The library was smoky but unscathed. The fire, it seemed, was still confined to the painting-room. Old Giles was groping at the opening to the stairs when Geoffrey appeared coughing and choking.

'Buckets,' he gasped. 'Buckets upstairs. Form a chain.'

Lady Ainsley took charge. Pails and pitchers had arrived

from everywhere—from stable and dairy and farm. Soon a constant relay was being passed, hand to hand, from Jenny toiling at the pump, to Geoffrey waiting at the head of the stairs to empty them into the room.

Little by little the smoke grew less. Water poured down the stairs and swept across the library floor. But at last the word was passed down the line, 'It's out.' Everybody stood still, gasping or chattering, till, at Lady Ainsley's word, the women, with wet bedraggled dresses, withdrew to the kitchen wing.

Elizabeth and Barbara clambered up the dripping stairs. At the top Geoffrey, with Lady Ainsley's hand on his shoulder, stood staring at the ruined room. Floor-boards, table and wainscoting were all charred and blackened. Geoffrey had torn down the burning hangings from the wall and they lay a sodden discoloured mass on the floor. Another few moments, he said, and the flames would have reached the rafters, and then nothing could have stopped them.

When he first came in the fire was burning on the middle of the floor. It was a kindled fire, a pile of papers, with the wooden easel and the picture propped over them and the red satin dress on top of all. Mercifully the oil and the paint were out of reach—that was why he had thrown them out of the window—they were so inflammable.

It was dreadfully clear that only one person could have kindled that fire. Lady Ainsley hastily asked Elizabeth where was Margot? Had she seen her?

Elizabeth shook her head. As she had passed she had noticed that Margot's bedroom was empty.

Lady Ainsley turned quickly and led the way downstairs.

They got only as far as the hall. Across the table on the dais Mad Margot was sprawled, sobbing as though her heart would break. As they came in she rose and flung herself at Lady Ainsley's feet.

She had done it, she cried. She had started the fire. She must have been mad. She could not remember anything. She only knew that she had lit the fire so that they could never desecrate that room again.

For the second time that day Lady Ainsley raised her, soothed and quieted her, and led her from the room.

The three left behind gazed at one another blankly. There

L 157

Caudle-mugs

was time now to realize how near to disaster they had been. Barbara's knees were shaking with excitement and cold. Her skirt was sodden, and when she looked at Geoffrey she saw that he was wet through. His face was black and smeared with smoke, and his shirt clung to him like a dirty rag. What could he do? He had no clothes here to change.

But, as if in answer to her question, old Giles came into the hall. He carried three silver caudle-mugs on a silver tray. My lady's orders, he said; Mr. Geoffrey was to be so good as to take a cup of caudle—and she had poured a little for Miss Elizabeth and Miss Barbara too, but they were to have no more because it was too strong for them. And afterwards they were to change their dresses. When Mr. Geoffrey had finished his caudle, her ladyship asked that he would take horse at once—in one of the master's riding cloaks—and ride to the Rectory for dry clothes. After he had changed, would he of his goodness ride on into Henley to fetch the apothecary for Madame Margot. Her ladyship thought that she should be bled at once to take down her distemper. The horse was being saddled now.

Geoffrey nodded. He applied himself promptly to his caudle cup, but he found it difficult to manage. It had a silver spout running up the side through which he had to suck up the caudle. The liquor caught his throat and made him cough, for it was hot spiced wine.

From the door old Giles came back. He had forgotten to say that her ladyship asked pardon for sending Master Geoffrey on an errand when he must be worn out, but the men were still away and she had no one else to send. And would he please come back to supper and stay the night?

Full of importance and good caudle, Geoffrey went off.

Barbara and Elizabeth took their drinks more slowly. Barbara remarked that it was very strong. Elizabeth nodded. She was fast recovering her normal cheerfulness. Grandmother's caudles were always strong—she put wheaten flummery and sugar and orange-flower water and goodness knows what else and mixed them with ale and wine. Father always said that Grandmother's caudle would put him under the table quicker than any sack.

Barbara giggled happily. Aunt Anne made caudle too—at least she called it cordial, but probably it was the same thing. Only it wasn't nearly so strong. Anyway she felt beautifully warm now. She had been very cold before.

The supper table

Their mugs empty they went upstairs to put on dry clothes. Though they tiptoed past Madame Margot's closed door Lady Ainsley heard them and came out, her finger to her lips.

Margot was sleeping, she said. But this time she would not leave her until the apothecary had been. She must have some blood let to quiet the tumult in her mind. When they had changed, they could tell Jenny to bring up the basins and the towels and all the usual things for the apothecary. Then they had better take their embroidery and sit quietly in the parlour until supper. They had had enough excitement for one day.

Geoffrey returned sooner than anyone expected. The apothecary came with him, and as they had not made more than average haste out from Henley, it was clear that he must have ridden in at breakneck speed.

Jenny brought in a gate-legged table and laid supper in the parlour—by her ladyship's orders, she said. Lady Ainsley, coming down later, said that everyone was too tired to make a fuss about a meal to-night. They would have just a dish of eggs and a manchet. Margot was sleeping. The apothecary thought that she would wake quite calm in the morning.

But even now the excitement of the day was not over.

Lady Ainsley had only just said the grace after meat when Jenny came hurrying into the parlour bearing a folded paper decorated with a red seal. A messenger had just ridden post-haste from London to bear this letter to my lady.

All eyes were fixed on Lady Ainsley. Barbara, sitting next to her, could not help reading the inscription on the outside of the letter.

To My Lady Ainsley at Ladybourne Hall.
    Haste, Haste, Haste!

Elizabeth, recognizing the seal, whispered, hoarse with excitement, 'From Father. It's from my father.'

They could hardly bear the suspense while Lady Ainsley read the letter. At the end she told Jenny that there was no reply. The messenger should be given a good supper and a bed. She would see him in the morning. In the meanwhile everyone should get to bed early so as to be up betimes. There would be much to do. Sir Humphrey was in London. He would be here to-morrow.

Jenny bobbed in acknowledgement of her orders. The messenger had gone on to the village, she said. He had letters also for Parson Hayward and for her mother at the Wheatsheaf.

The Wheatsheaf? Geoffrey and Barbara looked up expectantly. Did that mean that Father was coming too?

Lady Ainsley smiled at them. Yes, their father was coming down with Sir Humphrey in a hackney coach. Sir Humphrey had crossed Europe without touching France, and had shipped to Harwich from the Hague. He was very tired for he was not yet really strong after his fever. So he was hiring a coach. The roads were dry and hard now, and they should be here by the evening.

Elizabeth was bouncing about, as excitable as ever, and Barbara had a feeling that she and Geoffrey ought to be excited too. But Father's coming meant that they would have to go back to the Wheatsheaf. My lady said that Father sent a message about it. But they would have plenty of time to collect their things in the morning.

When she heard this Elizabeth stopped bouncing. Must Barbara really go? she asked. It would spoil everything if Barbara had to go away.

Barbara was not going a hundred miles, her grandmother told her, laughing. And perhaps, one never knew, before very long Barbara might be coming again. She squeezed Barbara's hand as she spoke. Then she turned to Geoffrey, and her voice became deeper and more serious.

She had not even begun to thank him for what he had done, she said. It was his presence of mind and his courage which had saved the old house and she would never never forget it. Then, as he kissed the hand she held out to him, she smiled again.

In fact, she said—and her voice was not quite steady—he might possibly save the old house twice. He had already saved it from burning—and perhaps, for all they could tell, he might even save it from being pulled down.

The Great House of the future

Chapter Eighteen

THE next morning Geoffrey and Barbara left the Hall.

They parted company at the gates. Geoffrey went back to the Parsonage to collect his things while Barbara went straight to the Wheatsheaf.

Mrs. Jarvis was delighted to see her. The place had seemed quiet, she declared. Her room was all ready. No one had used it while she was away. Oh, yes—and she would find a surprise waiting for her. It was lying on the bed.

A surprise? Barbara's curiosity awoke at once. What sort of a surprise?

Mrs. Jarvis's hearty laugh rang out.

Better go and see, she joked. Barbara was a bad girl, and she ought to have had a right good scolding.

Puzzled, Barbara climbed the little stairs.

On the bed lay the green sarcenet dress, clean, crisp and freshly ironed. Every sign of candle-fat had vanished and there was only just one tiny scorch mark on the front.

Barbara held it out to look at it. It was hard to realize that it was the same dress as the crumpled greasy bundle which she had pushed into the cupboard.

Suddenly she stopped dead, the dress suspended in the air. On the bed lay something else—something small and red, of knitted silk—Father's purse.

For a moment she stood gazing at it—hardly able to believe her eyes. Then she snatched it up, and hurried down the stairs.

Where did it come from? she cried to Mrs. Jarvis.

Mrs. Jarvis laughed. Come from? Out of the dress, of course—rolled right up in the middle of it. It seemed to be caught up on the hooks in front. Hadn't Barbara missed it? It was a lot of money for a little girl.

Barbara said at once that it wasn't hers. It was Father's. He had lost it. Then she thanked Mrs. Jarvis for getting the stains out of the dress, and ran outside to look for Geoffrey. She did not want to be asked any questions.

Geoffrey was just coming down the road from the village, his cloak bag over his shoulder. Barbara went to meet him, holding the purse behind her back.

She could not resist begging him to guess what she had got. It was a *nice* surprise, she reassured him.

But Geoffrey had too much on his mind for guessing, and told her so. Feeling a little snubbed, Barbara held her hand out in front of him—the purse lying in the palm.

Geoffrey stared at it, as though he had seen a ghost. Then gradually his whole face lighted up.

Where did it come from? he cried. Where on earth had she found it?

Barbara told him.

He nodded slowly as he listened. Of course. One could see it all now. She had been leaning over the cupboard, and probably he had pulled out the purse with the plans when the light was out. It was odd that she'd not found it when she changed, but it was dark, wasn't it?

Barbara nodded. Yes, it was dark. And, didn't he remember?—they'd done everything in a hurry.

Geoffrey did remember. What a mercy that they had not mentioned Ned. Just imagine—Ned would have been accused for nothing.

This hadn't occurred to Barbara. What a narrow escape it had been.

Another thought struck Geoffrey. Mrs. Jarvis did not know that the purse was missing. Obviously Father could not have mentioned it to her. That showed that he had made up his mind. He must have been quite certain that Geoffrey had taken it, otherwise he would have made inquiries. Well! This would show him! How grand to be able just to hand him the purse. Barbara would have to do that part. After all it had been hooked to *her* dress all the time.

Barbara was ready enough. She would enjoy it. But how about the rest of the story—the plans and the site and everything? They couldn't tell Father one part without telling him all. Geoffrey nodded thoughtfully. Yes, that was true. Anyway, he'd got to tell Father soon. He couldn't wait any longer because my lady would be sure to talk about it, and it would never do for Father to hear about it from someone else.

He'd choose the best time, and then he'd give a sign to Barbara and she could start off by handing Father the purse. After that Geoffrey would do the rest.

They spent the whole afternoon sitting on a gate and watching for the coach, but the sun had gone down behind the trees before the distant rumble of wheels told them that it was really coming. Quite stiff and tired of waiting, they jumped off the gate and stood at the corner where the cobbles led round to the front of the Wheatsheaf.

The coach, a light hackney with two horses, attended by Sir Humphrey's lackey on horseback, came bowling down the slope of the road at its best speed.

It stopped beside the inn. Barbara could see two faces inside. The nearest to her was Father, and beyond, a man wearing a monstrous fair periwig.

As Geoffrey sprang forward, Father stepped out. He turned to say a word of farewell, signed to Geoffrey to close the door, and the coach drove away.

Father was in excellent spirits. He was glad to be back, he said. London was intolerably hot, the smells were awful, and there was a plague of flies. Now that Sir Humphrey was home they'd be able at last to get on with the building at Lady-bourne. He was longing to see it started. It had hung fire too long.

Barbara looked at Geoffrey. Wasn't this his chance? The purse was tucked into her bodice, out of sight, and Geoffrey was to give her the sign when to produce it.

But Geoffrey shook his head. Father must sup first, he whispered. Barbara sighed. It was hard to wait.

Mrs. Jarvis laid the supper in the parlour, close to the open window. When at last Father pushed back his chair and began to fill his pipe, Geoffrey nodded at Barbara.

Father stepped out

The moment had come.

With her heart thumping, Barbara went to Father's side. She had something to show him, she said. Then, just as she had done before with Geoffrey, she opened her hand.

Father stared at the purse, amazement and relief in every line of his face. Where did she find it?

Barbara explained as clearly as she could. Nevertheless Father was still puzzled.

But what were they doing at the cupboard in the dark? he questioned. Why did they want the plans so urgently?

From that point, Geoffrey did the talking. He plunged straightway into the story of the site. He described it in detail, told how they had pegged it out and finally produced the sketches that he had made.

Father's astonishment grew with every moment. He examined the drawings, at first with a smile; but the smile gave place to a pucker of serious concentration.

At last he looked up.

Well, he remarked; Geoffrey had certainly succeeded in taking his breath away. Judging from the sketches their site looked remarkable—exactly the sort of place suited for a modern house. But Geoffrey had not realized that everything was settled already. Sir Humphrey had passed the plans for the new house on the ground of the old one. They were all ready to begin. It was too late now to talk about new sites.

Barbara could bear it no longer. She butted in.

But my lady had seen the site, she cried. My lady loved it. She was going to try and get Sir Humphrey to build the house there.

Father sat up. He looked startled. Was that true? he asked Geoffrey.

Geoffrey tried, rather unsuccessfully, to keep his voice from shaking with excitement. He replied that it was quite true.

Glancing outside at the closing darkness, Father said that it was too late to go out to-night. But obviously he must see this site of Geoffrey's. They should take him there first thing in the morning.

Geoffrey and Barbara were downstairs and waiting almost before the sun had risen over the hill. Father was up too, but he lingered talking to Mrs. Jarvis in the kitchen.

When at last he came outside and joined them, there was a peculiar expression on his face. He crossed the yard to Geoffrey.

Mrs. Jarvis, he said, had just been telling him about the fire at the Hall. He was very proud of Geoffrey—very proud indeed. In fact he was beginning to believe that he had rather a remarkable son.

There was a whole lot more of the story to be told to him— the part about Mad Margot and the painting-room, and it was Barbara's turn to do the talking. Geoffrey was too preoccupied in leading them across the Park so that Father might see the very best view at once.

The grass was soaked with dew, but neither Geoffrey nor Barbara thought about wet feet, and when they crested the hill and started to go down towards the site, Father forgot about wet feet too. The sun slanted sideways among the leaves, and through breaks in the trees they could see that shining crescent of river sweeping round the valley. Father said that it was in truth a lovely spot, but when suddenly he saw the plan of the Great House outlined in white stones in front of him, he stood silent in astonishment.

For the next hour he and Geoffrey worked together, planning and measuring. There were plenty of difficulties, Father said. But he thought they could be overcome. The two of them walked back to the Wheatsheaf deep in consultation, with their hands full of scraps of paper and notes. Father was almost as full of enthusiasm as either of his children, and he had to keep reminded himself that, after all, so far it was only a game. He had undertaken to build a new house on the site of the old one, and unless Sir Humphrey altered his mind, he would have to do it.

They had hardly finished changing out of their wet clothes when a messenger rode up from the Hall with a letter for Father. It begged him to come to dinner and to bring Geoffrey and Barbara with him.

Barbara dressed herself in her green sarcenet, feeling that it was years since she left the Hall instead of only yesterday. Walking up the drive was like going home.

Sir Humphrey, with his mother and Elizabeth, was out in the garden. He was a tall man, taller even than Father, and his fair periwig, the highest that Barbara had ever seen, was rather terrifying. But when he smiled his face was kind, and his eyes were of the same serene grey as Lady Ainsley's.

He asked Father, with an air of great ceremony, to present Geoffrey. He understood that it was this young man he had to thank that he had a roof over his head to-day. And, so he was told, he even had to consult him about the roof he would have over his head in the future.

Everybody laughed except Geoffrey who blushed violently.

Sir Humphrey patted him reassuringly on the shoulder.

He was a brave boy, he said, a very brave boy; and as for his house-planning in the Park, it was a prodigious bit of work. Elizabeth had taken him there. The children must have been very industrious. Their father had been taken to see it too, had he? Ah well, it seemed that they were both men who were ruled by their children. Anyway, they could discuss it all after dinner.

Dinner in the hall was a much more formal affair when Sir Humphrey was at home. Parson Hayward was there and said a very long grace, and the table on the dais seemed quite crowded with four grown-up people and three children. Madame Margot, Lady Ainsley told them, was much better, but she was to rest in her room for a few days.

The servants at the long tables were all very spruce and clean, and the usual hum of talk from the body of the hall was absent. It was so quiet that Barbara heard Sir Humphrey say under his breath to Father that he was not sure that he liked this ancient way of eating meals. When he got his new house, he'd have a dining-room, and live like a seventeenth-century gentleman and not like a patriarch.

They sat a long time, for Sir Humphrey had plenty to say about his European travels, but when at last they moved to the withdrawing room, he suggested that they should go out and have another look at this wonderful new site by the river. They could not all go. It should be four grown-ups and one expert—and he poked Geoffrey jokingly with his finger.

Barbara counted hastily. That meant Sir Humphrey and Father, my lady and Parson Hayward and, of course, Geoffrey. She and Elizabeth were to be left behind.

Lady Ainsley caught sight of her disappointed face, and came over to her. It was best like that, she whispered. They should hear all about it afterwards. And she'd got a lovely plan. Everybody was going to have a collation in the Park this evening. Yes—all of them—out of doors. It was a continental fashion that Sir Humphrey had liked. It was called a meal 'al fresco'—that meant 'in the fresh air'. The maids were getting everything prepared and they could both help to carry it out. Look—over there, under those big beeches in the shade. It must be all ready by the time the grown-ups got back.

Quite consoled Barbara and Elizabeth spent a busy afternoon backwards and forwards between the Hall and the beeches.

It was the most elaborate out-door party they had ever seen. Carpets and rugs were carried out and spread. There were cushions for the grown-ups to sit on, and delicious things to eat.

When it was all ready they were left in charge to see that everything was safe until the grown-ups arrived.

They did not have to wait very long before they saw them coming back across the Park. They were walking very slowly and were all deep in conversation; first Sir Humphrey and Father, with Geoffrey between them, and a little way behind, Lady Ainsley with Parson Hayward.

As they reached the shade they all threw themselves down, Sir Humphrey first helping his mother to a comfortable seat on a pile of cushions, and then mopping his hot face between the massive curls of his periwig.

It must be admitted, he said, that the new house would be pleasantly cool over there facing the river.

Barbara gasped and clutched Elizabeth's arm. 'The new house.' Did she notice? He said 'the new house'.

Lady Ainsley heard her and smiled at them. Poor children, they were on tenterhooks. She begged Sir Humphrey to be quick and tell them the news.

Sir Humphrey, his great length stretched on the ground, turned his lazy grey eyes towards them.

Well, if they must know, he had got a new architect—or rather there was a new partner in the firm of architects who were to build the house. They were now father and son. The new partner had persuaded him that a certain site, near the river, was the ideal spot for his new house—and he had agreed. To put it in plain English, the Great House was to be built on Geoffrey's site. That had a double advantage, because when he lived in the new house, his mother and Elizabeth could, if they preferred, continue to live in the old one.

Elizabeth jumped about excitedly. But her father had not finished.

Architects had to be paid, he said. And as he understood that the new architect's great ambition was to go to Oxford, he was going to arrange that for him by way of payment. Mr. Hayward gave a most hopeful account of Geoffrey's studies, and his father consented to his remaining as Mr. Hayward's pupil until he went to the university.

Barbara looked first at Geoffrey and then at her father. Father, smiling with pride, had slipped his arm across Geoffrey's shoulders and Geoffrey's scarlet face was lit with happiness.

It was true then. All that Geoffrey had hoped for was

going to happen. Barbara clapped her hands. She just could not help it. But the action drew all eyes to her.

Sir Humphrey smiled at her in his kindly way. He had been told, he said, of a little lady who had laboured up and down a hill with baskets of small white stones—her own idea too, if he was not mistaken—— He turned to his mother. Hadn't they some news for this little lady too?

Lady Ainsley spoke softly. She had meant to tell Barbara afterwards, she said. But since everything was being told now, there was no point in waiting. She was glad, she was *very* glad to say that Barbara's father had consented to allow her to remain with them—with herself and Elizabeth, at the old Hall, to share Elizabeth's lessons, and grow up with her, and be her friend. Would Barbara like that?

Barbara could not speak. She could only cling to the hand that Lady Ainsley stretched out to her. To help her my lady went on talking.

The family would not be parted, she said, for Father would be there very often to supervise the building of the new house, and Geoffrey would be at the Parsonage and, she hoped, often at the Hall. And perhaps her Aunt Anne would come and stay sometimes.

With her heart too full for words, Barbara gazed across the Park at the old Hall, lying mellow and gracious in the golden sunlight. Its long roof-tree stretched like a quiet horizon among the gables and chimneys. From the first moment that she saw it, she had loved it. And now it was to be her home.

But Geoffrey faced the other way, towards a grove of trees above the river. His eyes were fixed on the Great House of the future.

Postscript

ABOUT the Pictures: When you come to the end of the story, perhaps you will go back for another peep at the pictures; and if you do, you will probably find a good deal more in them than you saw at first glance. All the *things* in them are real—the actual articles that were generally used at that time. Nothing is made up. You can still see some of these things in use to-day. Others are found in museums or old houses. Some are only to be seen in old pictures.

If you look at the street scene at the beginning of Chapter I, you will be able to pick out some of the things which Barbara heard when she woke up that morning in London. There is the milkmaid delivering milk, the man carrying a sack of coal, the cobbles over which the ironshod wheels made such a clatter, the gutters down which the dirty water poured.

In the picture of the landing-stage down by the river (page 7) you can see old London Bridge, and St. Paul's half built and hidden in its scaffolding. The Monument which was just finished, is there; and the Tower is in the distance.

On page 8 are Aunt Anne's galoshes and Barbara's pattens. Galoshes are far older than the rubber overshoes which we call by that name to-day. In medieval times the words 'galoche' and 'patten' meant the same thing—a wooden clog sole. But by the seventeenth century galoshes had become more elaborate. Samuel Pepys in his diary mentions both pattens and galoshes. The iron galoshe illustrated here was a shape imported from France.

The picture of Chelsea Hospital on page 13 is taken from a print made soon after the building was finished. It looks different to-day simply because the trees have grown up and the Thames Embankment has been built up between it and the river.

At the beginning of Chapter III you can see a picture of traffic ploughing along a rough main road. Look at the coach and six, the huge carrier's wagon, with its round 'tilt-hood' stretched over hoops, which took passengers as well as goods, the country cart, the woman riding pillion, the packhorse carrying barrels, people walking—and notice that the man also wears a pack harness—and in the distance horsemen who have taken to the fields for greater speed. There is a closer view of a carrier's wagon on page 42 after it has delivered Barbara's trunk. Though it is so big and dark inside, you can discover some of the many loads, from a family party to a basket of ducks, which crawled round the country on those huge iron-shod wheels.

See how many objects you can spot in the blacksmith's shop on page 23 and then turn to the joiner's on page 39. There, if you look closely, you may find chairs and tables, a wheelbarrow, a cradle, a lot of 'barley sugar' baluster posts, and Father's cupboard right at the end. The tall flat paddles in the shadows on the left are for controlling the water at the river weir—you can see them in use in the picture on page 56. On the joiner's bench is a vice, and various tools and saws. The big saw for cutting lengthways through tall tree trunks is shown on page 47. You will see that it has a wooden frame to keep it straight. In real life the log would probably have been laid more horizontally across the pit, but in the drawing it is propped up so that you can see the man down below pushing on the saw.

There is a lot to look at in the picture of the kitchen on page 60. Notice the bacon hanging from the rafters, the gridiron for grilling meat hanging on the wall, the family Bible on the chest, the door of the bread oven beyond the fireplace with a second opening inside the chimney where the embers were emptied, and the bundle of faggots standing all ready. The shovel and scoop for taking the loaves out of the oven show best in the illustration on page 62 of Barbara making bread.

You get a closer view of the same fireplace on page 88. In this picture chickens and other good things are roasting on the spit, turned by means of a smoke valve in the chimney; see the little wheel and driving belt at the far end of the spit; the dripping falls into the tins below. Over the fire a frying-pan with a very long handle is suspended by means of a sliding ratchet from a bar which will swing round as required. The big cauldron for hot water hangs as usual by its hook and chain from a crossbeam in the chimney. A warm drink in a mug is heating on the top of one of the andirons, and at the back you can see a small portable oven standing on a trivet.

On page 69 the illustration shows how rushlight tapers were made. The wick—usually the pith of a rush—was laid across the long-handled dipper and lowered into a pan of hot tallow or fat. Each dip was hung to cool before being given a second coat. It must have been a messy business and it is small wonder that the smell of the steam made Barbara feel sick.

The scene inside the church on page 80 has a great deal of detail, but probably you, like Barbara, will look first at the hour-glass beside the pulpit, which tells the preacher when it is time for his sermon to end. Up in the gallery the musicians have some strange instruments. There is a fiddle, not unlike a modern one, a bass viol, very like a violincello, (you will find a close-up of a similar viol on page 94), a bassoon at the back, and a sort of recorder on the extreme right. The man in the middle with a thing like a trumpet is using a vamp-horn, which was hardly a musical instrument at all, but a megaphone into which the leader of the band sang the tune—a sort of primitive loud-speaker. Probably you know the phrase 'to *vamp* an accompaniment'.

An inkstand, quill pens—with the penknife for shaping them, a canister of sand for drying the ink before the invention of blotting-paper, candlesticks and a pair of snuffers for trimming candle-wicks, sealing-wax and a seal—all these appear on page 100. But you may find more amusing still the picture of Eliza-beth's toys on page 105. Every one of them is taken from some picture of the time—skipping-rope, kite, battledore and shuttle-cock and all the rest. You can see this actual doll (a better portrait appears on page 53) in the Victoria and Albert Museum in London. The high chair is in the same museum. So is Elizabeth's desk (page 140).

There is plenty to look at in the picture of the still-room on page 108, especially the primitive arrangement for distilling essences, the pestle and mortar on the table, and many other things, most of which you can probably recognize for yourself.

The basket-making on page 114 contains the picture of a fish kiddle, or trap, lying on the ground on the left. (You have heard the expression 'a nice *kettle* of fish'). It is not unlike a big lobster pot and was used in much the same way.

On page 126 the collection of clay pipes are gathered in a strange-looking iron rack. The purpose of the rack was to stand the pipes in the hot embers of the kitchen fire so that the foul and blackened clay was burned as white and fresh as when they were new.

Finally, you will find below the picture of a gateway, the old watergate of Essex House which used to stand with other great mansions in the Strand. The old gateway remained at the bottom of Essex Street where the publishers of this book have their offices, until it was damaged by air-raids and demolished at last during the printing of these pages. Laurence Irving drew it for the firm of Methuen as their Colophon or sign. It was through this gateway that Barbara (see p. 10) ran on her way to the river.